Writing Places

Writing Places is a creative writing and literary translation project exploring the connections between writing and place in Kolkata and Norwich.

It is a partnership between the National Centre for Writing, the University of East Anglia, the British Centre for Literary Translation (BCLT), the Kolkata Literary Meet, Seagull Books and the Centre for the Translation of Indian Literatures at Jadavpur University.

It is supported by the British Council and Arts Council England ReImagine India fund as part of the UK–India Year of Culture.

Writing Places

TEXTS, RHYTHMS, IMAGES

EDITED BY
ARUNAVA SINHA

LONDON NEW YORK CALCUTTA

This project is supported by

Seagull Books, 2019

ISBN 978 0 8574 2 732 8
Texts and photographs © Individual authors and photographers

British Library Cataloguing-in-Publication Data
A catalogue record for this book is available from the British Library

Typeset and designed by Sunandini Banerjee, Seagull Books, Calcutta
Printed and bound by Hyam Enterprises, Calcutta

CONTENTS

Your Ticket

ARUNAVA SINHA

'Where are you?'

No question is heard more often when eavesdropping on mobile phone conversations—and really, do we have a choice any more but to be part of other people's information exchanges?—and perhaps no sentence unwittingly captures the duality of spatial existence for the twenty-first-century individual. There you may be, feet firmly planted on the ageing asphalt of a Kolkata street, but your attention could be roving over the Scottish hillside where a social media friend is hang-gliding and posting a video. With updates from every conceivable combination of latitudes and longitudes flowing into our second life on that tiny screen, can we really answer that question up there with any degree of honesty any more?

Still, as everyone who has ever made a social media post—a text update, a photograph or even a set of wordless emojis—after arriving in a new place, or returning to an old one, knows that there is an almost primal need to convey or even broadcast the contours of one's relationship with a place. Whether it's occupied physically or emotionally, whether it is home or three thousand light years away, whether it is amongst sensations as familiar as a favourite piece of music or as novel as, well, an unread novel, no artist can quite resist bringing into their art something of the place that they're in.

When there are places, there must be journeys. No matter whether the distance covered is physical or emotional, all writing is a journey, a record of or a meditation on the flows and eddies and diversions and landslides of ideas, happenings and people, of birth, death and life, of love, longing and losing, of fact, fantasy and fiction. And journeys are just where the book you're holding in your hands began—though of the predictable kind, the ones that involve suitcases and passports, maps and phone alarms, expectations and disappointment, discoveries and disasters.

Over the past three years, these journeys have been taking the writers and photographers whose work is featured in this book, over hills and plains and across rivers and seas, between India and England, and, through all this, on tours of their imagination as well. Being the artists that they are, each of them has turned to their preferred medium—from short stories to photography, from historical investigations to academic analysis, from poetry to reportage—to create or to contribute, especially for this collection, a special work. It is these works—an anthology of idiosyncracies and memories, constant sleight-of-hand of the imagination and of observation, and a (sometimes whimsical, sometimes determined) commitment to telling stories, in words and in images—that provide the itinerary of the inner journey of *Writing Places*.

Have a good trip!

The Gentlemen of Bengal

LUCY HUGHES-HALLETT

At the end of a week of book-talk in Calcutta (literary festival, translators' workshop, symposium) I moved to a village in the Bengali countryside, not far from the Ganges. There a late-eighteenth-century *rajbari* (lordly house) has been transformed into a hotel, and there I met Mr M.

I saw him first from the upper verandah. He came into the rajbari's neoclassical courtyard through the vaulted passageway leading out towards the pond where metre-long monitor lizards bask in the mud. His posture was notable. He is not tall, but he carries himself as a person to whom one is required to look up. He wore a white dhoti and kurta with a fawn waistcoat. He is fastidious about his appearance. I was later to notice the complicated artistry with which his still-plentiful hair had been cut. He is, as he was soon to tell me, a septuagenarian: Mr M takes pleasure in polysyllables.

The hotel staff were setting up the charpoy on which, later on that evening, the deaf-and-blind singer would sit cross-legged, wearing dark glasses with his chilli-red robe. They were arranging clay oil lamps on the broad stone steps that lead up to the house's grand portico. They do this every evening, and surely know how it's to be done. Nonetheless Mr M oversaw, directing proceedings with small movements of his hands, like those with which a British shepherd issues commands to his dogs.

New guests arrived—a businessman from Calcutta (petrochemicals) accompanied by a young woman a foot taller than him in her spike-heeled ankle boots. Mr M greeted them with stately gestures. I didn't know who he was. I'd already met the hotel's proprietor. He's a very different character, a Punjabi antique dealer turned Calcutta big-businessman, who bought the rajbari a decade ago when it was a roof-less wreck, and has restored it, the biggest and most beautiful piece in his collection of bric-a-brac. But whoever might actually own this place, Mr M was playing host.

As evening falls in the village, a great clangour arises from the cluster of temples across the pond (most of them derelict and much over-grown, one still in use). The evening prayer—signalled by temple bell and metal drum and conch. Inside the rajbari the oil lamps are lit and a similar hullaballoo arises. The staff—three very young women in red and ivory-coloured sarees, three men sharply dressed in dark trousers and shirts—line the steps. Mr M ascends to the portico and there, in a ringing voice, intones a prayer, first in Sanskrit and then in English.

Shantih Shantih Shantih. Peace Peace Peace. He follows up the ancient invocation with a prayer of his own devising, for tolerance. It is all very impressive, and as the attendants process afterwards through the colonnades, conch blaring, drums banging, aromatic smoke wafting from the swinging brazier, it is splendidly theatrical.

I was watching from a raised terrace at the end of the courtyard. By the time the procession and the holy smoke reached me, Mr M was there too. His sacred duties discharged, he set to work with equal assiduity on performing his social ones.

He sat very upright on the edge of the divan on which I was lolling with my Kindle and a fresh-lime soda. He told me of his passion for Wordsworth's poetry, and gave me a brief lecture on the therapeutic properties of the local flora. He talked of his daughter's recent marriage: it was an arranged, match, he said, and the bridegroom was gratifyingly tall, 'nearly six foot,' with a promising career. He talked of how his family, who once owned not only this palatial building but also many others, and vast tracts of land besides, had lost it all.

Their own indolence was largely to blame, he said. Their forebear had been granted the estate by Emperor Akbar four centuries ago. His descendants had lived idly off it ever since. Then there were the conventions governing inheritance (no primogeniture) which meant that by the time the hotel's owner found the Rajbari it was co-owned by seventeen members of the M family, several of whom were locked in feuds with several others. And there were the communists who ruled West Bengal for thirty-four years until 2011, confiscating much privately owned land. All these things had contributed to the fall of the house of M.

I mmmed and oh-reallyed but my contributions to the conversation were not really required. Mr M explained that he lives in an annex of the rajbari. He graciously accepted a share of my pakoras. Then he said abruptly, 'Now I must give my company to others,' and he moved away across the terrace, shoulders well back, white clothes glimmering in the lamp-light, conferring his company as a favour on the hotel's other guests.

I was there for five days. I saw him often. If I crossed the courtyard in the late afternoon he would be ensconced on a wrought-iron bench entertaining one or two other local gentlemen who looked as though they were also septuagenarian, or octogenarian or in one case more likely nonagenarian.

One morning he took me on a round of calls. We travelled by auto-rickshaw along the narrow brick-paved paths leading off into the watery delta countryside, where green or rust-coloured ponds cover as much of the terrain as the mango groves and garden-plots and expanses of meadowland grazed by tiny black goats.

We stopped at a house whose balustraded balconies and high arched windows and stucco pilasters were stately, but which was oddly truncated. A cousin of Mr M's lived in a part of it. The other half of the house had belonged to an uncle who had demolished it rather than share. The cousin's sitting room was as grandly proportioned as the rajbari's rooms, but while they are now painted ivory white, to please the internationally uniform modern taste for pale decor, this room was painted, as most of the village houses are, in brilliant shades of magenta and turquoise and lime green and saffron yellow. A woman was sitting cross-legged on the floor dicing a cauliflower when we came in: she gathered herself up and disappeared behind a bead curtain. A portrait, an oil painting which might have been by Zoffany, hung on the wall above the television. Beneath it was a photograph of a teenager with the same long nose as the portrait's subject, looking solemn in school uniform. A tiny boy with the same nose followed us inquisitively.

Our next stop was a rectangle of green the size of a cricket pitch. Once an ornamental lake, now entirely covered in water hyacinth, it was part of a garden. On an island in its centre stood a circular gazebo. At the end was another pavilion, neoclassically pillared. Both structures had lost their roofs, but Mr M remembers coming there with his uncles as a child, and how they would cross the now-vanished bridge to the island to sit at their ease in the shade while musicians played and dancing girls performed in the far pavilion. As he reminisced, a woman came past, a bundle of firewood strapped to her back. She hesitated, and looked anxious. He spoke to her, and after she had gone, a goat trotting behind her, he explained that she had been afraid he would be angry with her for trespassing on what was once land reserved for his family's private pleasure.

Finally we called on his friend, a widower with a small house but a large garden containing over a dozen varieties of dianthus, and many magnificent dahlias, each one carefully staked. The friend cut a papaya from a tree and sliced it and served it to us with great ceremony on enamelled tin plates. Mr M sat in a faded plastic chair pulled slightly forward, so that he faced away from us, his deferential courtiers. He pulled a piece of paper from his breast pocket. It was a poem, of his own authorship. He declaimed. We murmured our admiration. Mr M then led us around the garden (its owner following meekly) explaining the medicinal uses of each plant.

It was a delightful morning. I was pleased that Mr M had judged me—or so I supposed—worthy to be shown the remnants of his family's lost domain. The next day I saw another hotel guest setting out with him. Later she described her outing. It was precisely the same as mine had been. Meeting Mr M's cousin and his gardening-friend, eating the papaya, hearing the poem, it is all part of a treat routinely on offer as part of the hotel's service.

Mr M interested me because he was charismatic and entertaining, but also because I believed I recognised him. I know this situation, I thought. This is Chekhov. Or, this is the sequel to Chekhov. This is how Madame Ranevsky might have conducted herself, if Lopakhin, having bought her property and cut down her cherry orchard, had invited her back to live in the house that was once hers, so that she could amuse his visitors and give the place a bit of aristocratic tone and a connection with a less mercantile, more romantic past. Or, this is how Uncle Vanya might have ended his days had his brother-in-law's estate been sold to a businessman who turned it into a hotel. The fact that Russia's aristocracy would be ruined by a communist revolution, only thirteen years after *The Cherry Orchard's* first performance, set up other echoes. Bengal's communist regime was not Soviet in its structure, but the Ms have been dispossessed, as Chekhov's ennui-enervated, land-owning gentry were to be, by followers of Karl Marx.

So I thought—idly, enjoyably, but with a shameful lack of rigour. Literature provides templates that help us to understand the situations we encounter in the real world. But it can also mislead. One of the things readers learn from fiction—the most subtle fiction anyway—is that people are not types. Each one is unique. And each one exists within a situation whose variables are so many that no one life exactly replicates another.

I do not know—because it would have been impolite to ask—on what basis Mr M lives at the rajbari. Is he an employee? A tenant? A squatter? Or a privileged guest? Unquestionably, his presence in the hotel adds to its charm, but is he being exploited or indulged? Who is doing whom a favour here? I don't know the answers, and there's a great deal more I don't know. My knowledge of Bengali history is a mere smattering picked up in a two-week stay. I don't know how much cor-respondence there is between the way the politics of class played out during the late twentieth century here in Bengal, and nearly a century earlier in Russia, a country I've never visited. Rather than seizing on broad resemblances, might it not be more illuminating to look for minute variations? In Calcutta I had been taking part in a seminar at Presidency University, where there was much talk of the 'universal' and the 'specific' in literature. It was generally agreed that the former is a dodgy concept, now generally discredited. *Autre temps, autre pays, autres moeurs.*

*

The symposium was convened by Jon Cook and Amit Chaudhuri. As well as being a novelist, a musician and a professor of literature both at the University of East Anglia and at Kolkata's Presidency University, Chaudhuri is an advocate for the idiosyncratic architecture of South Calcutta. Part Bauhaus, part art deco, the houses which were built here in the 1920s and 30s are elegant and exuberant at once—modernist without any of modernism's usual austerity, their clean, curving lines ornamented with wrought-iron sunbursts and lotuses and zigzags, their balconies elaborate.

The symposium over, Chaudhuri led a group of us on a walk around the area. This is the part of town in which his first novel, *A Strange and Sublime Address*, is set. In it a small boy from Mumbai spends the summers with his uncle's family in Kolkata. The uncle, Chhotomama, and the rest of his family are observed from the point of view of the observant, wondering child. The boy in the novel is called Sandeep, but Chaudhuri doesn't deny the book's strongly autobiographical nature.

We turned into a quiet street. A couple of men sat chatting on a bench. Trees cast a pleasant shade. This, explained Amit, is where his uncle lived, though the house described in the novel has been demolished to make way for a block of flats. We walked a little further. The row of houses was interrupted by an unobtrusive low-rise building. An elderly gentleman was sitting on the first-floor balcony, leaning back in a rattan chair, reading a newspaper.

'That's my uncle,' said Amit. His face in repose is serious, even lugubrious-looking, but now it lit up. He was gleeful. 'It's my uncle,' he kept repeating. 'He doesn't know we're here. That's him! My uncle.' We looked up. There was Chhotomama, stepped out of the pages of a book, a fictional character made flesh, with spectacles slipping down his nose. A breach had been made in the membrane separating fiction from reality. It was a deliciously transgressive moment. We all laughed, a bit nervously, as though we had had a small but agreeable shock. We stared, and then we stole away.

*

Mr M has created a fictional role for himself—one that probably corresponds pretty closely to his private self, but which is nonetheless artificial. Playing that part is his job, or his hobby. He puts on a show. Amit Chaudhuri's uncle is a real person with a life in the real world, but there are thousands of readers who know his fictional simulacrum, who are fond of him, or amused or exasperated by him, without, in reality, knowing him at all.

It was only as I was leaving for home that it dawned on me that I had been so struck by encounters with these two people because I have been thinking for a long while about those who coexist with fictional versions of themselves. My first book, *Cleopatra*, was about the way the few documented historical facts about an ancient queen have been distorted to make for her a great range of imaginary personae—the femme fatale, the exotic temptress, the ruthless autocrat, the clinging mistress, the noble suicide. And here is a passage from my last book, *The Pike*, about Gabriele d'Annunzio, the proto-fascist poet and master of the art of self-promotion:

> *d'Annunzio was to become that oddly disjunct thing, a celebrity, and he well understood the difference between the person and the 'idol', the persona fame foisted on him. In old age he was to write feelingly of the 'horror of being "Gabriele d'Annunzio"'.*

Finally, this is from the novel I had recently finished when I set off for Calcutta. The novel is set, over three centuries, in a great house (the English equivalent of a rajbari). In this passage it is 1989, and Flora, a young woman who part-owns the house, has made a career as a studiedly eccentric television personality, presenting popular documentaries about stately home life. Coincidentally, it is a visitor from the subcontinent (the part that is now Pakistan) who comments.

> *Selim crossed the grass and squatted beside them. Nell nodded towards the baby and put a fore-finger to her lips.*
>
> *The crowd of technicians walked backwards ahead of Flora as she progressed slowly along the herbaceous border, her long skirt brushing against the catmint and valerian, locks of hair tumbling from her striped silk head-wrap. As she came closer her voice carried to them over the shoulder of the soundman who was holding a boom beside her face. The camera trundled on silent wheels.*

'Fertilisation you see . . . insemination by ruffled taffeta . . .
Absolutely ENORMOUS hooped skirts . . . could hide anything,
I mean, LOVERS, chamber pots . . .'

The procession passed on into the yew passage.

'Flora is very interesting,' said Selim, forgetting the injunction
to silence. 'In my part of the world people have been amusing out-
siders by making themselves into imitations of themselves for
centuries, but for the British I think it is a new thing.'

I'd crossed the world, from Britain to Bengal. I'd met new people, been party to stimulating discussions, yet I was still thinking about the same old things. Cultures and societies may be so various that literary universality is a chimera, but the observing eye, and the mind behind it, will find their favourite material wherever they are set down. '*Caelum non animum mutant qui trans mare currunt*,' wrote Horace. They change their sky, not their soul, who run across the sea.

A Table Two Feet in Diameter

PIA GHOSH-ROY

As soon as I stepped out of the taxi, I was ready to go back the thirteen hours I had travelled. Between Calcutta and Kolkata, the house hadn't changed a brick. The same robust structure, well maintained and unbeautiful. Its long yellow balcony filled with rows of towels, sarees and salwar-kameezes, drying, dancing, telling the world that there were lives being lived in that house, baths being taken, clothes being washed, pegged, dried, folded, repeated. On that clothesline hung the daily tickings of a household. Reassuring routineness wired to neighbours, vendors and passers-by so they knew when you'd taken your bath, when your maid took the day off so no clothes were washed, when you'd bought a new saree and its colour ran, when you first changed to under-wired bras because your sister sent a bagful of them from abroad. They knew when someone died and his clothes were never washed again, and they knew when a daughter came home to visit. The clothesline told them before anyone else did, and tomorrow morning everyone would know that I was here.

I could hear their elbows speaking in nudges. *There's that daughter, the younger one, you know, the one who is living with an Englishman in London.*

I didn't live with an Englishman, and I didn't live in London. I lived in Norwich with David who was part French-Irish and part what he liked to call Mongrel-Mash. But to our neighbours in Kolkata, any place in England was London, and any white man in it, English.

The door opened as I paid off the taxi. Didi walked out. *Ah, now there's the older one. The one who said no to Harvard and Yale to take care of her parents. Really, a girl like diamond.*

*

Didi looked tired. Her eyes were lined with kohl and shadows, smudges of half-moons that hollowed her face. How I'd missed her! She was the one who tugged me back home more times than I cared to come.

Baba's death five years ago had changed the sturdy rectangle of our family like a car whose wheel had rolled off mid-drive. Sometimes it felt like we were still parked by the roadside waiting for help.

Baba had been my part of the pair, Ma was Didi's. Without Baba to balance my end of the seesaw, I was thrown off kilter, unsure of how to edge myself closer to the only parent I had left, unsure of whether I even wanted to. That—along with my relationship with Kolkata, which forever teetered between love and avoidance—made me stay away longer. I found excuses to cancel my visits in December, I found a busier job, I found David.

'How is she?' I asked into Didi's hair as I held her tight. She smelled of cooking and sleeplessness.

'Still the same,' she replied. 'Thank god you're here now. She's been asking for you all morning.'

The taxi driver's sharp honk made us pull apart. I dragged my suitcase off the seat and pushed the door shut. In this city, patience was by-the-meter and annoyance freely dispersed.

'Is anyone else here?' I asked, pulling my suitcase with one hand and slipping the other into Didi's, our fingers linking like hair in a braid.

'Na. Some of the neighbours were here to see Ma, but I told them she had to rest. You'll want to see her without everyone looking on.'

I let my head drop on her shoulder, relieved. That should buy me a few hours before the next conveyor belt of visitors started passing through. Some would come to see Ma, but many to see the NRI daughter who lived a life too far away to monitor from their windows.

'Thanks, Didi,' I said, giving her a squeeze. 'Love you.'

'Hmm,' Didi smiled, smoothing an imaginary crease on my sleeve, replying in the only way she knew how.

Declarations of love were not for Didi. 'This emotional verbosity of the Americanised', as she called it, made her shift in her seat— emotions were for arms and eyes and actions to show, not for lips to speak. Even on the phone, my *Love you, Didi!* would usually be answered with a *Hmm, bhalo thakish*, keep well, take care.

When I first moved to England, my phone conversations with Didi used to leave me with a sense of wanting. I was alone in a new country and hungry for words that could ease the distance. But when the words came, Didi's love was always swathed in concern like gauze on a cut: *Have you eaten? Don't stay up too late. Why are you coughing? Don't eat all that greasy food.* By the end of the conversation, her worries would leave us both exhausted.

Didi mothered me like Ma mothered her. With time, she even started sounding like Ma, their words had the same ebb and flow. It was easy to confuse them on the phone. David, poor man, could never tell them apart. He hadn't met Didi yet, but he knew more about her, and my life in Kolkata, than any man I had been with before.

I didn't talk about that life much any more. I had learned that talking about India could sometimes turn into an exercise in social self-defence. I grew weary of the reactions its politics or customs could throw up—a raised eyebrow, a polite laugh, a confused shake of the head, opinions dressed as questions. *Having people cook and clean for you, isn't that modern-day slavery?* I became alert to conversations that might stray to cows and caste system, rapes and lynching, the slums, the slums, the poverty, the slums. When you come from a country of complicated coarseness, an ugly beauty, where there is so much right and wrong at the same time, you often find yourself at the end or the beginning of an explanation.

A few months into my life in Norwich, I remember joining a friend's family for Sunday lunch at The Red Lion, where her father, while carefully cutting his roast, had apologized for his curiosity, but he'd always wondered if people in India still used their hands to wash their bottoms. And—no offence—was it the left hand or the right, since they also used their hands to eat with, didn't they? 'Maaark!' his wife had scolded, her exasperated laugh as old and ineffective as separate Hot and Cold taps in a British loo. No no, Mark had said in reply to his wife's admonishment—he was curious that's all, genuinely interested, really, no offence intended. It's just that his parents had had very little money, you see, so he did know all about hard times. But even in rationed Britain in the middle of a war people had managed to find old newspapers to do the job with, thank goodness.

David came as a relief. He was unruffled by differences. Everything was okay. Everyone was a fellow-traveller. Just people. Made up of thoughts and messy lives that didn't need categorizing. He'd grown up between divorced parents, two good people who found it impossible to be good together. He had two sets of clothes and shoes in two houses, and an understanding that most people were just trying to do the best they could. He travelled widely, mixed indiscriminately, read hungrily and was not caught off-guard by the the world I grew up in.

*

Every window in the house was shut, curtains drawn to keep out the angry afternoon sun. I left the suitcase by the door and slipped off my shoes before wading across the shadows to Ma's bedroom door. This too was shut. I could hear the drone of the air-conditioner on the other side. Cold air slipped out from under the door like lithe ghosts.

'She's sleeping,' Didi whispered. 'Don't wake her just yet. She's had a difficult night.'

I backed away, glad that I had to wait, ashamed that I wanted to wait. Didi had taken care of everything. She had gone through months of hospitals and doctors, soothed Ma after her chemotherapy, watched her fade out, come back and start to fade out again. All I had to do was put a face to the change, see her in her wasted body. All I had to do was not have the shock sprout on my face like weeds in a garden.

Sometimes, I wanted to be in Didi's place, walking parallel to Ma's gradual decline. Her image in my head not preserved like a childhood drawing, but changing as she changed, shrivelling as she shrivelled, rotting as she rotted. I wanted this, secure in the knowledge that it would not happen. Didi was there. I'd slipped out through a back alley, skirted around reality, to Norwich where I lived with a framed photograph of Ma with thick wavy hair, young skin and straight back, standing in the kitchen in a starched saree, about to teach us how to make luchi on a Sunday morning.

You can't be a timid cook, she used to say, handing us a rolling pin and a sieved metal spatula. Timid cooks are terrible cooks. Hold the spatula firmly, like that. There. Now slide the luchi into the oil, yes, good. Na, na, if you want your luchi to puff up, don't let it come up for air. Push it down into the oil—yes, like that—it'll puff up and push back at you, see.

The old kitchen had been replaced with a new one a few years ago. Glossy black cabinets with neat chrome handles sat above a granite worktop, at odds with the rest of the house. I'd seen the new kitchen on my last visit, enthused over it dutifully, but once back in Norwich my mind had changed it back to the old one, so that when I imagined Ma or Didi pottering around, it was always in the kitchen where I had fried my first luchi, amidst pale-yellow walls with peeling distemper showing a mossy green underneath.

Didi, on the other hand, didn't suffer from such bouts of sentimentality; she never had. Maybe you needed to leave home to hanker for the ordinariness of old things. In my first few years in England, I had not missed much of my life in India. I'd missed Didi, Baba and Ma, but phone calls were often enough to take care of that. Their life remained reassuringly plain and familiar. My weekly updates, on the other hand, were filled with awe at my shiny new foreign life. It had the sound of cheap souvenirs clanking around a metal box.

'Baba, you'd love the supermarkets here, so clean! You wouldn't have to walk holding your trousers up. Oh, and I've started going for morning walks like you . . . autumn mornings are so beautiful here! Yes, yes, I'm careful, you don't get mugged here, that's only in London.'

'Ma, I'm going to York with some friends on Saturday. By coach. Na, not that kind of coach! A long-distance bus. It's called coach here.

The friends? No, they're British. Yes, *British* British. What else? Oh, Brit Indians and Indian Indians . . . let's just say the twain don't meet.'

'Didi, guess what? I cooked a meal for Amy and Jo the other day. Haan, they *loved* it! They've never really had proper Indian food before . . . just the rubbish you get here, you know . . . Chicken *Balti*. Whatever that is.'

Life had been too full of change, too full of loud observations, to think about missing India. That came a few years later. When the grey English skies started to seep into my veins and I felt the need for sun and sound and chaos rise through me, like milk forgotten on a hot stove, spilling out and flowing and frothing over things I had not missed before. The smells of Kolkata, loud, humid and tangy. The sounds of home—slippers slapping on mosaic floors, pressure cookers hissing in other houses, the whir of the ceiling-fan, a dog barking, a procession protesting, stories on the streets.

But even as I missed the city, it was not a missing that left me unhappy. I almost enjoyed this yearning, this yearning for a known place in unknown ways. I knew nothing could airbrush a place to perfection better than nostalgia.

'You go freshen up,' said Didi, heading towards the kitchen. 'There's a towel and a roll of toilet paper on the bed. I'll make you some tea.'

'Na, Didi. Think I'll wait for Ma to wake up, then take a shower,' I said, following her into the kitchen. 'If I go into the bedroom now, I'll just want to sleep. My body thinks it's 3 a.m.'

I sat down at the small round table next to the kitchen window. The window had a deep sill, further extended with a metal grille of knots and crosses. On my last visit, the grille had been painted a chalky white. Now rust pushed its way out of spots where the paint had bubbled.

This used to be my hideaway. This is where I sat, my bottom on the metal grillr tingling with the knowledge that there was nothing underneath. Sometimes, I would hang an old bedcover printed with elephants holding tails in a circle, and shut my alcove off from the rest of the house. I spent hours here, playing with stainless-steel bowls and spoons, while Ma, Baba and Didi moved around like shadow-puppets on the other side of my world.

Between games, I would watch the neat file of black ants travelling from one end of the sill to another, each carrying crumbs of food larger than themselves. I watched their efficient queueing, took note of how they worked, how two ants crossing each other from opposite directions stopped to nuzzle and greet before carrying on. Their greetings polite yet perfunctory, programmed by unquestioned instincts. Sometimes, I would lower a bowl face down in the middle of their row and break up their well-behaved queue. This made them lose all sense of place. They ran helter-skelter, and did not return for several hours. Their queues defined them. Without it they were disoriented, unable to work. I did not know then that I would learn to live by similar, orderly queues in a new country years later.

The window sill was different now: pots of moneyplants sat where I used to. Their undemanding roots and heart-shaped leaves trying to lure in luck and wealth through the knots and crosses of the grille. We sat down at the breakfast table with our mugs of tea and talked. Didi told me about Ma's medication, and why it had to be changed a few days ago. She told me about Ma's meals, the long sessions of coaxing and scolding, threats of the ICU and of tubes up her nose if she didn't eat. She told me about Ma's bowels, her bursts of anger, the bedsore on the right side of her lower hip, the new night-nurse who would join on Friday.

Ma hated being cleaned and fed by strangers, but I'd managed to convince Didi to get a nurse for the nights. Given Ma's moods, however, no one could tell how long the nurse would last.

I asked questions to keep Didi talking. I was afraid that when she stopped, it would be my turn to speak. *Now, enough about this,* she would say, *tell me how things are with you.* What would I tell her? Would I start with the fantastic promotion at work? About David asking me to marry him? About the engagement ring I'd slipped off on the plane? My weekend wine-dine-and-draw workshops? Or that we were converting our loft into the library I'd always dreamed of?

Till last year, Didi had been a senior editor at the largest selling English daily in the city, a powerful voice in political journalism. She'd given it all up to take care of Ma. For the last few months, she'd been wading through doctors and appointments, figuring out ways to manage Ma's moods, learning to wash her without hurting sore spots. While I'd been in England perfecting the fine art of balancing Life and Guilt.

But this balance was easier to maintain when I was sitting thousands of miles away. The table between us now, this table by the kitchen window, was only two feet in diameter. From here, I could see more than I wanted to. I could see Didi's eyes rest on the pendant that David had given me on my birthday, then flick away. I could see her look at my French-manicured nails, and curl her own fingers in. I could see her withdraw without moving an inch.

After we finished talking about Ma, there was a new silence between us, pierced with unspoken splinters. She asked me nothing, not a single question about home, my work, nothing about David. She got up, took our mugs to the sink and turned on the tap.

'Didi, let me do tha—'

'Na, it's fine . . . sit.'

As she washed the mugs—slowly, taking longer than she needed to, pushing the soapy sponge in and out, round and round, holding each mug under the tap, filling and emptying, filling and emptying—I saw her shoulders soften. And I wondered how she had brought herself around. Did she have to imagine me as a child so she could go on loving me as an adult? What did it cost her, this unconditional love?

'I think I hear Ma waking up,' Didi said, walking over to my chair. She stroked my hair back, bent down and dropped a kiss on my forehead. '*Ja*, you go and sit with her. I'll make her tea and come.'

POETRY

Six Poems and a Postscript

TIFFANY ATKINSON

Wire-seller, Lal Bazar

who smiles from the kerb
like a man loosed from thought   who
when he feels its small tug   will turn slowly   fit his spectacles
& from the tangled afternoon   pull down
between his fingertips   its single filament

Kalighat

Sarah brings Kali
Fierce in her embroidered shawl she sticks her tongue out
From the temple she has carried in insurgence   somehow
Women all   we measure the distance in silence
between power   and what passes in the speaking life   for power

Yoga

Early-morning gym-companion / business-man / mid-
forties / white shirt pressed and hanging by the showers/
folds / unfolds himself like something being born / still
nine parts liquid one part hurt / he brings the body stretching
into light / We nod and smile / I'm chugging out my tenth mile
on the treadmill / You go very far he says / yes far indeed / but
tell me can you bend

The poem Kolkata[1]

Amit too   I read   between landings
has considered poetry's irrelevance

Like certain genres   certain cities too
become unviable at certain points in history

Just look at poetry   A tale of near-extinction
O   give me any city that's unviable

& push me out in just what I stand up in
Here on a holy-day quayside   for example

I can only move anywhere at the molecular level
A mote of me jangles with the bright girls up the temple steps

Another rises on a drift of puja smoke
Another bombs a couple's grinning selfie with its weird eye

One part strips & wades into the river
& a bit of me dissolves into the marigolds   those threaded suns

A fragment sizzles off the skillet on a mustard seed
Another shatters from the ferry bell   alighting

1 Italicised text from Amit Chaudhuri's *Calcutta: Two Years in the City* (Union Books, 2013).

on a lolling dog who twitches & rolls over   onto
bits of me that burnt down to the ground a century ago

Another million bits fly out   attached to kites   not going
anywhere   like most joys   like a lot of language actually   like this

Parable

Arnab and Shonali feed us
sweet fish steamed in leaves with mustard seed

I cast aside my awkward knife and fork
& suck my steaming fingers   Now I'm not one

to discourse on the authentic but **THIS FISH**
Shonali says that all Bengali mothers make this

Arnab grins   ask anyone   All week I follow women
with my notebook
                    Never mind   says Paramita

when in Norwich six months later I attempt
by way of welcome   fish *paturi*   with a sullen Nordic cod
and mustard from our claggy fields   A boon!   our host says

for the cats   & thus we all decamp for lunch at the White Horse

which though implicitly a Brexit pub   (George cross, a signed pic
of Prince Charles above the bar)   is nonetheless the best roast

east of London   so   implausibly   come Spring I find myself
once more on a Kolkata rooftop eating canapés   what *luck*

until the deputy-high-commissioner's wife takes me aside
& says   the fish!   Oh lord a diplomatic incident   I think

but really she just wants to say it's all about the seed
which is a mother's true advice   Did no-one show me

& she leads me to her kitchen

                              It's a culinary story
rather feminine in scale   but still   the massed historic

city leans in   on a woman wrapping mustard seed
in silver foil   with all its horns   and all its flowers   blaring

Postscript

Almost I don't go
        because of a family grief and in winter of some kinds
it's hard to imagine
a whole other continent
Don't be absurd says my sensible friend   just step over your-
        self

GALLERY

light.together

TEXT AND PHOTOGRAPHS BY PARNI RAY

Dear P,

Thanks for the postcard, the colours look beautiful.

It has been very hot here. Last night I shifted the bed against the window to catch the breeze. I hadn't switched the light on so this morning the room was in disarray. A rectangle of dust lay exposed on the floor, where the bed had been. Remember that old smoking pipe we turned the house upside down looking for? And the hardback edition of the Iliad you pinched from your best friend's boyfriend? They were there.

Today I think I will empty out the cupboard on the staircase landing. Who knows what's in there.

Love, S

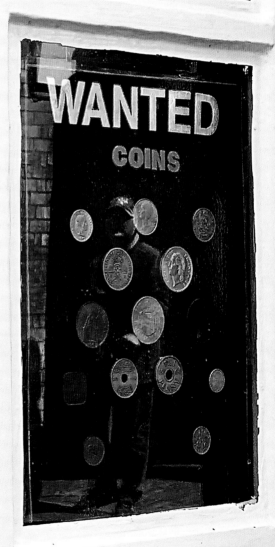

Dear P,

A part of the ceiling in the kitchen fell off today. It fell into the pot I had on the stove. Very messy.

While cleaning up I looked up at the hole it had left behind. It reminded me of Australia, the way it appears in maps.

The kitchen is a health hazard now so I have shifted the stove to the living room. This morning I ate eggs and toast and last night's potatoes. What have you been eating?

Love, S

Dear P,

New neighbours shifted in next door. I should have guessed, there was hammering all of last week. Renovations probably. A few days back the owners had dropped by (remember the man with the glass eye?). I had wondered about it then. When was the last time they came by? Who knows. Their old tenants had been quiet recently, no more fights. The kids were all grown up too. Where did they move to, who knows.

Anyway, they brought in the new furniture this morning. I watched them unload the lorry from the verandah. So many mattresses, stacked like they were waiting for the princess to climb up.

Love, S

Dear P,

There has been no light at home since yesterday. I used the electric cooker again and the fuse blew . . . I tried to fix it but appear to have done something wrong. I went down to the mains with a torch, but it was locked. The red and green cables were all tangled up behind the wire square on the box. When I tried to look in closer I caught a mouthful of dust and came up sneezing.

I suppose I have to call someone soon. Tomorrow, maybe. Good thing it's winter and there are enough candles at home.

Love, S

Dear P,

Haven't heard from you in a while so took out all the pictures you sent.

You aren't in any of them. How is one to know if you really were in those places amidst all those people?

Dear P,

There was to be a meteor shower last night so I went up to the terrace, after years.

The nightscape has changed. There is a big floodlight at the end of the road now. Like a UFO it illuminates everything. The lights on the bridge are now red, then purple. There are new buildings, steep and tall, their lights drown out others I once knew.

The new neighbours have curtains, orange patterns on red. But the others—remember the house with the green walls?—their windows are still open and unadorned. Their television was on, a flickering blue square in the bright green square that was the window.

I sat watching and waiting for the meteors. It got chilly so I came down to get covers. Must have dozed off at some point. When I woke the sky was clearing, I was sitting leaning against the water tank.

The lights were still on . . .

MEMOIR

Hare Street

VESNA GOLDSWORTHY

'So in the streets of Calcutta,

I sometimes imagine myself a foreigner . . .'

Rabindranath Tagore, *My Reminiscences*

It would have been quicker to walk. The taxi takes an hour to cover two and a half miles and there is no excuse for the lack of speed. The streets are empty, as empty as the streets of Calcutta get. Soon enough everything will begin to rise: the temperature, the dust, the noise. The pavement dwellers are stirring in the last cool gasps of darkness. Some spend their nights on charpoys under awnings made of tarpaulin or cardboard; others on bare concrete, as though they fainted in the middle of a walk. Even homelessness has its hierarchies here.

I have been in Calcutta for five days, long enough to feel the points of tension between my English words and their meanings in this city. Homelessness does not seem right. The sleepers occupy their patches with more confidence than I have about belonging anywhere. They run their businesses of mendicancy, or of repairing trinkets which would not be worth mending anywhere else, and they reside on the premises, as it were, more happily than the homeless in London. Then again, my perception may be the effect of warmth and mid-January sun. Or, perhaps, there is so much destitution around me that I have to recalibrate the measurement of empathy in order to be able to step out at all.

My powers of description become unanchored in Calcutta. In the weeks which follow my short journey I embark on an endless series of false starts, until I lose my bearings and no longer know how to frame the story. Why begin with the homeless? I am told that Mother Teresa is the city's mixed blessing: the global icon of charity who—long before you arrive—makes you imagine Calcutta as a place of misery. While I walk its streets, the city seems anything but.

And it is not just my writing that gets unsettled. I feel on edge one second—there are too many people, too many cars, too many buildings, too much smog, too much clatter, too much, just too much of everything clamouring for my attention. I can't wait to go back to an England which seems from here a dream of green luminosity and peace. The next moment some inner membrane bursts and I float along the same streets, relishing the glowing colours and scents of hundreds of unknown oils and spices. I don't want to go back to bland, black-and-white London, ever. I want to stay in Calcutta.

A couple of months later that feeling recurs when I least expect it. I miss Calcutta. I want to go back. And I don't know how to make sense of that desire.

The jetlag does not help. It hits me five days into the journey, just when I think that I got off lightly. On the sixth night I fail to fall asleep. When the darkness starts thinning, soon after five thirty, I decide to visit Hare Street.

*

The battered yellow taxi feels like the cars of my East European childhood; drafty and makeshift, like something barely converted for the purpose. It takes to the road like a pair of bicycles soldered together yet threatening to go their separate ways with each bump and every pothole.

When I hail it I shout 'Hare Street', the RP way—non-Rhotic—the pronunciation I have been using for decades. *Heaahh Street.* To be sure I am understood, I repeat it in my Serbian voice, rolling my Rs like pebbles, to form the sounds of someone visiting Britain for the first time next Thursday. *Herrr Strit.* I unfold the map. I point. See here? Yes?

Haré Street, the driver repeats, pronouncing the name like the Great Mantra, not even glancing at my piece of paper, as though he has not an atom of a dilemma, as though this, taking European women to Hare Street, is what he does at dawn every dawn. Haré, as in Hare Krishna.

For the first mile or so our ride seems simple enough. The Victoria Memorial glints palely and soldiers rehearse their drill for Army Day on the Maidan. I read the map like a piece of concrete poetry. Streets named after families I recognise—Russell Street, Lindsay Street, Dufferin Road, Bentinck Street, Princep Street—alternate with those whose sounds scan like a nursery rhyme: Sido Kanu Dahar, Moti Sil, Chowringhee. Others recall the streetscapes of my own childhood: Lenin Sarani, Marx Engels Beethi. Like the city itself, the names reflect a world in which nothing is thrown away and everything is endlessly recycled.

Then, just as we are almost there, the zigzagging begins. We turn into side streets and stop for minutes at a time. The driver shouts *Hare Street* at passersby. Men step into the road and, looking at me all the time, lean inside the vehicle to give intricate directions to the place which must be less than half a mile away. Haré, I hear, again and again. Haré. Haré.

I catch our momentary locations on the map, then lose them. We get closer to Hare Street, we drive away. The meter ticks its way to three hundred rupees—the equivalent of three pounds. The driver gets engaged in a lengthy exchange with two men on a moped. There is a lot of pointing in every direction. I move as if to open the car door, and offer to drive the vehicle myself. I don't mean it. I am well aware that I am being taken for a ride in more than the literal sense, but I don't mind. In a city of polyglot Anglophones much more fluent than I, not one of the men my driver stops seems to speak English. They all smile wide, reassuring smiles, like extras who had spent days on their agreed spots waiting for this particular cue.

I relax and watch the glorious facades unfurl by the window. At least the language of the architecture is abundantly familiar. I know this place, I think. I have known this place all my life. Calcutta is the place I have always seen between sleeping and waking. The lines come, unbidden and misremembered, from Rebecca West's account of her visit to Yugoslavia in *Black Lamb and Grey Falcon*. They describe a sense of returning which sometimes hits us in a place we have never been to before, a recognition of something archetypal in it which chimes with our own sense of being. For me, this *déjà vu* in Calcutta speaks of an encounter with the East—not the Orientalist fantasy of languor and desire, but a vision of a partly Occidentalised East, whose image somehow simultaneously speaks of childhood and decrepitude. I have studied such images long enough to be wary of the false analogy, to mistrust my own eyes. Yet what I keep thinking about Calcutta is that it is London's half-sister. A visit to it feels like time-travel, but I am not sure if it is London's past or London's future that I am seeing.

*

In his twenties, my father-in-law was a young officer in the Guides Cavalry in the final days of the Raj. The last in a sequence of Goldsworthy males who served in India, I know he loved the sub-continent at least as much as he loved England. When he died in 1999, we inherited his library. There were more books than we could house in our London home, but we kept a selection of his India volumes which now sit by my desk alongside the cheap editions of European classics I purchased as a student of comparative literature at the University of Belgrade.

My favourite among my father-in-law's books is the *New Calcutta Directory* for 1857. Two volumes, enormous in spite of the thin Bible paper they were printed on, list the city's inhabitants, street by street, house by house. The entry for Hare Street, on page seventy-nine of the second tome, records fifteen buildings and their dwellers. No. 8 has the German Club, with 'F. Schiller, honorary secretary and treasurer'. The occupant of No. 9 is listed as 'A. Mitchell, merchant, distillery, chemical and rectifying works'. At No. 10 I find 'Goldsworthy and co., banking and general agents. Thos. Goldsworthy, firm of ditto. W.T. Goldsworthy, assistant in the bank of bengal (sic). Degumber Mittre, silk and corah manufacturer, &c'. No. 11 houses the French Consulate, 12 an optician, a chronometer maker, a firm of milliners and a professor of dental surgery. How can one not find a book like this, with its thousands of implicit, untold stories, a literary Pompeii, a compulsive read?

Yet the records were out of date as soon as the books were published. It was one of those years. Walter Goldsworthy, my great-grandfather-in-law, started his brief banking career at sixteen and ended it at twenty. His father's business was far from flourishing and Walter wasn't a natural pen-pusher. With his eighteen-year-old brother Roger and a friend by the name of James Erskine, Walter abandoned his clerical duties and rode to avenge the events at Cawnpore amid the terrible crisis that is now variously known as the Indian Mutiny, the Sepoys' Rebellion, and India's First War of Independence.

The second half of the nineteenth century proved glorious for the two Goldsworthy boys. It was an explosion of the sort of upward mobility they might have dreamed of when they left their modest London home, a rented house in St John's Wood, in their mid-teens: a kind of rapid progression that seems barely imaginable even today. Both were given commissions without purchase in fashionable cavalry regiments. Walter became a general and, in 1885, the first MP for Hammersmith. His brother became in turn the governor of Saint Lucia, British Honduras, was knighted, and finally, though this does not sound like a promotion (and, word has it, it was not), the Falkland Islands. India was the making of them, in military rather than monetary terms. Even their sister made a good marriage to a well-connected officer serving there.

Hare Street is a point of departure: in the 1850s, it wasn't where the smart set resided any more than it is today. I am the first family member in several decades to have gone back, yet this 'back' is a misnomer. My native country was part of a different empire—the Ottoman one. My paternal ancestors, then still living in the barren uplands of Herzegovina, could not have achieved imperial distinction in the 1850s without converting to Islam. And Walter belonged to the political party which sustained the Porte like a patient in a coma. What am I supposed to feel on visiting Hare Street?

In some ways, my native Balkans now seem much more postcolonial than India, with a host of new countries and a wavering sense of direction and destiny. Britain played a major role in dismantling my country of birth only twenty years ago; its moralistic muscle is not a matter of some barely remembered past.

India has moved on. It is now a global power which sees Britain courting its patronage and trade. When I speak to people in Calcutta, the history of British imperialism seems to matter mainly to the chattering equivalents of Islingtonites, whose houses and apartments are grand and servants numerous, while the masters remain as Anglo-centric in their grievances as they are in their education. Used to having it both ways, they talk of Oxford and Cambridge at cocktail parties and literary soirees, and are not apologetic about their privileges in the way their current British counterparts are. I admit it: I am jealous and distrustful of that sense of righteousness and justice which you need in order to occupy the moral high ground. Walter and Roger would have had it too. I keep changing my mind.

*

The spire of St John's Church, the old cathedral, comes into view, like a stubbier, more solid version of St Martin-in-the-Fields. When I finally get out of the car, I tip the driver, although I am aware that I should hardly be encouraging this approach to his job.

The gardens are freshly watered. I am alone, amid a profusion of flowering plants whose names I have no idea of and for the entire hour I spend inside the church. There is a large Zoffany painting of the Last Supper, freshly restored with German money, which features an array of Calcutta's residents of the late 1700s. Judas has the face of a Scottish auctioneer and Jesus that of a Greek priest. There are countless memorial plaques.

I could be in Cheltenham, but for the sun which streams through the high windows and swims under the domes with a faint coral, un-English blush, and for the narratives of lives lost early and cruelly, from cholera, diphtheria, typhoid and malnourishment. Walter and Roger took a hundred and forty days to sail to Calcutta. It took me barely longer than it takes to get to Cheltenham. I watched an in-flight movie, a Russian romantic comedy about Moscow couples honeymooning in Cuba, then slept the rest of the way. Is it surprising that I need a while to catch up with myself, that I start making sense of Calcutta long after I have left it, uncertainly piecing together the meaning of my visit?

In one corner of the church, almost obscured by the pews, I spot a plaque to James Erskine. At Lucknow, he was less lucky than my forebears-in-law were, a boy who never returned to Blighty. At that stage I know nothing about James. Later, I hunt his story down in the vast encyclopaedia of the dead that the virtual space now provides. He died at the hospital in Lucknow on 14 November 1857 from a musket shot wound received a couple of months earlier. Like Walter and Roger, he was serving with the Volunteer Cavalry under Sir James Outram. He was twenty-one and the third son of John Erskine of Elambazar (now Ilambazar), West Bengal, a manufacturer of sugar and indigo and the owner of a large shellac factory.

Alone inside St John's I feel an almost pulsating sense of a different Britain, much more distant than India feels now. Although I have lived amid its vestiges for the past thirty years, this Britain is alien and abstract, as if powered by potent energies which seem irreducible to human desires for wealth and adventure, although there is no shortage of those. For all my interest in Victorian culture, I might just as easily have married an Italian descendant of some Roman centurion who had marched from Puglia to Carlisle.

I leave the cathedral and turn the corner into Hare Street. I no longer remember which number I should be looking for. I do know that finding the right house will tell me nothing. There are one or two elegant, dilapidated villas which might have survived the 1850s, but they are on the wrong side of the street. No. 8 is a telephone exchange, a distinguished-looking edifice in dark salmon stone, old, yet not nearly old enough. No. 10 houses a Fedex office.

Hare Street is full of men. I am distracting them from their business. Although no one troubles me, I feel watched and on stage. I am observed so intently that I can't look at anything properly myself. I take a lot of blurry photographs as though the act of taking pictures can somehow excuse and explain my uninvited presence. I had intended to walk down to the Strand and the Hooghly but I lose the will. If there are ghosts on Hare Street, they are not speaking to me.

He is still where I left him although I never asked him to wait. 'Good?' he asks as he jumps out of the car and holds the door open for me, a huge smile on his face.

'Good,' I say and get inside.

A Phenotype

SOMRITA URNI GANGULY

'Calcutta reminds me of Trieste,' Philippe once told me. 'A beautiful, rich, old woman, now forgotten and lonely.' Philippe landed in Calcutta for the first time the year in which I was born. We did not know back then that nearly three decades later we would be walking down the crowded, cobbled streets of Meena Bazar in the stale, ancient, moth-eaten city of Dilli, under twilight skies that change colours like old lovers, talking about his exhilaration on sighting the port of Calcutta, and my solace on seeing the last of this land disappear behind the clouds. Philippe came to Calcutta from France, via Vietnam, in 1990. I was headed to New York City, via Hong Kong, in 2009.

'Trieste was the main harbour of the Austro-Hungarian empire,' Philippe said, one evening in 2017. 'It was a large empire, sprawling over all of central Europe, but its access to the sea was limited. Trieste was a sea-city and the only big harbour in this ageing empire. This made Trieste powerful and rich, much more than the size of the city betrays. And it was very cosmopolitan for its dimensions. Then, the empire was dissolved after the First World War and Trieste ended up being a part of Italy, on the western front, but for most of the century the city was just the Iron Curtain separating Western and Communist Europe. Soon, it was isolated and forgotten. But when you visit the city now you feel that once upon a time it must have been a thriving centre of power and activity. She's still rich, but very, very quiet.'

'You talk like someone from a dream,' I replied, thinking about the colonial past of my birthplace, about Job Charnock and Charles Eyre choosing this spot where Calcutta stands, over all other places, about the Portuguese and Armenian and British mariners who once called this distant, alien land Golgotha—from where, some say, my city got its name—but who nonetheless sailed to its perilous shores in the. seventeenth century. 'You talk like someone from a dream, and for a moment you made me feel sad for Trieste, as though she were a real person. I think I will die like Trieste: rich, alone, forgotten.'

'And beautiful then. Because Trieste is beautiful. Like Calcutta,' Philippe had reassured me.

Calcutta knows all my firsts. The first stolen D. H. Lawrence read under the torchlight of a Nokia 1200 mobile phone, way past bedtime.

The first time the engine of a car revved to life under my unsteady hands. The first time a beagle licked my fingers. The first time I bought a cigarette, armed with zero experience, and quixotic notions of adulthood. My friend and I, all of eighteen, walked for 2 kilometres after college to a fairly desolate area. We had fumbled and faltered while asking the wayside paan-waala for a Marlboro. It was the only name that both of us knew then. After that adult purchase, we walked down Free School Street, lined with old books and gramophone records, looking for a suitable hideout. We eventually reached the sanctum sanctorum of Hogg's Market, which swallows people into its great bowels, with overpowering stenches of barrels of unsold pigs' cheeks, dumped behind shops which had spotlessly clean front doors. We eventually took shelter in an abandoned church on Sudder Street, to hide from the rain and our shame of not having found a corner of space where we could experience our rite de passage. No matter where you go in Calcutta, curious eyes will be your constant companions. The cigarette was soggy by that time, lying in the back-pocket of my skintight denims, a symbol of our aborted, orchestrated plan of growing wings like butterflies, tired of our caterpillar lives. We took a kaali-peeli taxi back home, the second-best adult thing to do in 2008, our lips tasting of pomegranate lip balms when they should have tasted of burnt tobacco. The Ambassador taxi, with its galloping meter, had driven us from Park Street, via Esplanade, to Tiretti Bazaar and Poddar Court, and then on to Sovabajar, and finally Ahiritola, past Shyambajar. My friend Madhabi lived in an old North Calcutta house in those days.

She lives in Bombay now. How quickly she had disappeared behind the anonymity that the crumbling edifices of Calcutta 700005 can offer. Anyone can come to Calcutta from anywhere and melt into the city.

On hot summer afternoons, the lanes and by-lanes of North Calcutta sleep, like the owners of the red-brick buildings situated there. At other times, of the day and the year, these lanes are abuzz with children playing gully cricket; hand-drawn rickshaws; fresh markets; pharmacies, many pharmacies, well-stocked on Gelusil, Digene, Crocin and Calpol; confectionaries selling hot, spongy, syrupy, sweet rosho-gollas, and frying radhaballabis in cauldrons full of spluttering mustard oil; barking stray dogs; women, wearing baggy maxis or loose nighties, screaming obscenities, in jest, at each other across courtyards; super-annuated men sitting on charpoys playing card games at noon; young students making beelines for the local food carts selling egg-rolls and greasy chicken chowmein; and overflowing side-drains, choking with stale scales of fish, rotting vegetable peels and left-over rice.

The old houses, some of them a hundred years old, stand tall, though bent, as reminders of Calcutta's lost glory and heritage. Some of these houses have little banyan trees growing roots inside moss infected walls. Some others have money plants drooping out of broken, stained-glass windows. Some houses stand arrogant, distinct from their neighbours, recently repaired and painted in loud, bright, garish shades of strawberry pink or lemon-tart yellow. Their insides, though, are largely the same—voices whispering in kitchens; the calm routine of salt and sea smelling smoke coming out of the exhausts; unassuming rooms, with the plaster falling off in places; narrow, steep stairs leading up to an open terrace; red-cemented floors on which people still sit down cross-legged to eat their large meals; calendars of Kali or Krishna smirking from pegs hammered into arbitrarily chosen spots on the walls; four-poster beds with mosquito nets and soft bolsters; grey, sweat-stained curtains; and infinitely patient, infinitely proud, infinitely suffering faces.

The aroma of mutton being cooked in ghee and a thick paste of ginger, garlic and onions, greets people on the roads of North Calcutta every Sunday morning. The sound of Rabindrasangeet or Nazrulgeeti drifting out of half open, inviting, trusting doors, lures the tourist, the traveller, the misfit and the wanderer, walking down those lanes on dark, lonely evenings. Usually. That day in 2008, however, was different for me.

The children had all gone home. I had seen the dust on the make-shift badminton court that they were playing on settle down. The plastic slide had stood in solitary splendour. The swing had continued swaying on its own, its hinges screeching because of the rust. As I was navigating my way out of Madhabi's paara, a young girl, her hair wrapped in a wet white-and-red checked cotton towel, had come out on the balcony of one of the quiet, three-storied houses. She had put the washed clothes out to dry. Twelve yards of wet, soft cotton had been folded twice before being put out on the line. Beads of water had dropped on my hair from the fraying, free ends of that saree as I had stood under the hanging balcony briefly, looking up at the young girl. I had dreamt of snowflakes alighting imperceptibly on my eyelashes from a carmine sky but tropical, middle-class Calcutta offered me only the smell of Sunlight detergent powder. A cream-coloured pyjama, a blue-and-green checked lungi, a white vest and a couple of white handkerchiefs had been put out on the line one after another: one peg for two pieces of clothing, to secure them from flying away. Calcutta, they say, believes in sharing. The lungi, I had noticed, was particularly well worn. It had spoken to me of the evenings when the korta of the house must have returned from his ten to five government job, stepped out of the unnecessary socks, belt and corduroy trousers, and wrapped the checked cotton lungi around his waist like a long skirt, sat himself down on an easy chair, feet propped up on the side table, waiting for the wife to serve him the hot telebhaja that he had brought on his way back from work, with some shukno muri and cha. The telebhaja, thin slices of potato or eggplant soaked in batter and deep fried in oil, is unhealthy, of course, for a man of fifty. It leads to acidity, doctors in Calcutta are quick to caution. These general physicians know that a Bangali digestive tract is more fragile and inflammable than a Bangali ego. The wife, therefore, would probably always give her husband some shukno muri with the telebhaja. The dry puffed rice would help to balance out the ill effects of those oil-drenched snacks.

The girl had freed her wet hair from the gamchha. She had bent her torso forward and lowered her head such that her long hair was all in front of her face, baring her slender brown neck. She had twisted the towel into a rope and then beat her wet hair with it, as if dusting off the extra crystals of water from her locks. The spray on my face from the girl's hair had smelled of Lifebuoy soap, Dettol diluted with water, and faint coconut oil.

I walked back to the main road, thinking about how I was more fond of the Bangla word 'gamchha'—is it a diminutive of 'gaa'mochha', meaning 'wiping oneself dry'?—than the English word 'towel'.

'Maashi, shaak lagbe? Kolmi shaak? Palong shaak? Shojne shaak? O maashi?' The shrill voice of a young woman had wandered from one lane to another, like me, piercing the silence of that deserted afternoon in North Calcutta. The voice had taken me back to a play that I had acted in when I was nine. I was a rose-vendor, walking down the streets of London in that rendition of *Oliver Twist*, singing, 'Who will buy my sweet red roses? Two blooms for a penny! Any milk today, mistress? Who will buy my sweet red roses?' Only, that vendor in Calcutta had not been play-acting like I once had. It was her job. She sold edible leafy greens for a living.

Calcutta is aware of all my firsts. The first love letter (still unsent). The first poem (still unpublished). The first dream (still unrealized). The first kiss. At Eden Gardens. Under a light drizzle, standing behind a row of atasi bushes, with drunk fireflies for company, fluttering their Tinker-Bell wings relentlessly, restlessly, maddeningly. In that dot of a moment, I had felt infinite. I had convinced myself that love is forever. But Calcutta knows better. Calcutta knows not only of my very first kiss but of the several first kisses with the several people that came and went later.

I left Calcutta at a time when the city had nothing else to offer me, returning annually for three weeks, to get healed, or for lessons in humility. When I feel young, confident, beautiful, I choose places like Manhattan, South Delhi, West London. The list of reasons to leave Calcutta is endlessly long when you are growing up. The list of reasons to love Calcutta catches you by surprise by raising its hesitant head when you have grown up, when your heart has flown from mountain to sea to city to person, when you are weary of chasing fame and failure, and you long to be home.

I am home. I have been here for the last eight months now, and Calcutta has accepted me with a warmth that I have known nowhere else. It is easy to fall in pace, and in love, with the excruciatingly slow, relaxed, complacent life that this city offers. Is it healthy, though? I shall never know. But what I do know is that life cannot be all that bad as long as I can catch a ferry from Baghbajar Ghat at sunset and set sail down the Ganges with nowhere in particular to go and no one in particular to meet.

The Bourne Legacy

SHREYA SEN-HANDLEY

If you aren't Indian, you would have read about it as the ghastly 'Mutiny of 1857', the appalling overreaction of Indian soldiers to a lard-greased slip-up in the cartridge department. Indians however, prefer to call it the 'First War of Independence', that first blow struck by India against its British oppressors who had subjected them to indignities much greater than lardy cartridges over centuries of violence and pillage. If we take the middle ground and call it an 'uprising', we are still left with hundreds of thousands dead, cities scarred and villages razed to the ground. With the exception of the British casualties at the start, they were all Indian, all slaughtered in retaliation to the rebellion of a few thousand soldiers, and all in the name of imposing order. After this whirlwind of vengeance that the British unleashed upon the land, they shut themselves in the grand houses they'd built upon it, driving the wedge between the two factions deeper. The Indians seemed to withdraw from the fray too in response, leaving a landscape desolate of hope or harmony.

When the dust from the conflict had settled, what was left were the tales of atrocities committed in its course, which travelled far and wide. When these accounts, especially those about Indian reprisals against the British, arrived at the British Isles, they had an unusually unsettling effect on its denizens. If the first war's quelling temporarily dampened the Indian ardour for freedom, if the British thumbscrews put on Indian independence advocates so hobbled them for a while they appeared to have given up (not so, independence efforts of a non-violent nature were just ten years away), then the opposite was true of the English. It galvanised them, bringing them to the Indian cause and Indian shores in droves. These newcomers to the land had come not so much to suppress rebellion (though reinforcements for the army did arrive by the boatloads) but to rubberneck, castigate and memorialise the mutiny. A handful came to explain India to an audience back home both seething with fury and fascinated by its enigma. There was an intense desire amongst the British to know India and not know it at the same time. They wanted to understand it only so far as they could pigeonhole it, and, by reducing it to a cipher, own it more comfortably. Those who came across were cut from the same cloth; adventurous versions of the ones who sat at home wondering. 'I don't know what effect these men will have upon the enemy,' Lord Arthur Wellesley might well have said of them, 'but, by God, they frighten me.'

Such a man was Samuel Bourne, clergyman's son and banking clerk from Nottingham, who stepped on to Indian soil in 1863 with a different array of accoutrements than might have been expected—a sliding and folding camera, metal tripod and wet collodion photographic plates amongst them. Like his ocean-crossing comrades, he was not there to save the situation, nor to improve relations between the warring sides even slightly. But he was amongst the first to step ashore to tell the tale of British India through the relatively new medium of photographs. A tale that would be heavily tinged with his British presuppositions and Christian prejudices, as his first thoughts on arrival, on the 'sufferings of so many of his countrymen', proved. Yet like many other Englishmen of his time, he had this new strain in his character mixed in with the predisposition to be distrustful of the different; it was the urge to discover. And having discovered, to conquer. As with most of his kind, he marvelled at the sheer scale and plenty of India—in riches, spices and adventures—but was just as convinced that no other place on earth could match their 'green and pleasant' land. But he was shrewder and more observant. Fascinated by the vastly different landscape and naturally brilliant light, he was certain he could become a better photographer in those conditions (he hadn't forgotten after all the sting of prominent Victorian photographer George Shadbolt's criticism of his work as 'deficient in the artistic element'). And as beautiful as he believed

Blighty to be, he knew it lacked that essential ingredient which went into the most arresting pictures, 'The more brilliant the sunshine, the more I love to see the image on the ground glass; and arriving just fresh from England, where the dampness and the thickness of the atmosphere so sadly mar the brilliancy and crispness of the picture, I have frequently stood transported. What are all the obstacles to be overcome in comparison with the marvellous brilliancy poured over every surrounding object? If he could only transport English scenery under these exquisite skies, what pictures would he not produce!'

Nevertheless, Bourne was ill at ease in India and his early trip to Delhi deepened his discomfort. Bustling and hot with its large, low buildings and long, snaking streets baking in the sun, it still seemed to give off the scent of discontent brewed in the mutiny. And a palpable sense of danger, judging by his account, 'Delhi was a name, sadly, famous to every Englishman. You look on its threatening Red Fort and you scuttle, clearly.' Because he hurried on to Simla, the British Raj's favourite hill station, where he was reunited with the all-day drizzle and relative solitude of the Middle England he loved. The cool weather and white faces of the expatriate community there were such a relief after the hurly-burly of Delhi that he was almost complimentary about it, averring that, despite the 'disappointment its first sight gave me, it is not to be condemned. As regards the climate, nothing could be finer, one should be thankful to know that one has escaped that frightful heat which has been laying man and beast prostrate in the plains'. The colonial buildings mushrooming on the hillsides were British in appearance, with turns in the mall after meals and elaborate tea-time rituals to further comfort a homesick Bourne, he stopped feeling out-of-sorts. So he girded those loins and got to work. Taking care to avoid 'the mass of tumble-down native dwellings', he was able to take 'a considerable number of pictures of a certain class'. He even, on request, deigned to take group photos of the expat men and women; with parasols and cricket bats and servants lurking behind them. Staring stonily at the camera which was the norm at the time, the Britons looked only slightly more animated, hinting at their robust country-annexing proclivities, than the Indians, who were so studiedly stolid they barely appeared human. Which, of course, Bourne stage-managed to ensure the biggest volume of sales both in Simla and British settlements beyond. Bourne was already learning to mint money from shaping the British-Indian image to his customers' liking.

Yet Bourne wasn't in India for its people at all, whatever their colour. It was the hills he loved and thathe captured with pioneering clarity. But bigger and more compelling challenges were soon in his sights and it wasn't long before he was on his way to the Himalayas. This austere and majestic range with all the romance of the Alps, but much grander and more dramatic, had a particular hold on the European imagination. In 1843, Surveyor General of India George Everest and his team measured the peaks of the Himalayas and found them to be the highest in the world. That the tallest mountains were not in Europe was disconcerting, but as they were rather too large to shift, the British announced their 'discovery' instead in 1856, naming them with great fanfare after themselves. Bourne thought of another way of owning this magnificent mountain range. Between 1863 and 1866, he would photograph it more extensively than any other photographer. On his three trips into the Himalayas, the final one lasting six months, he captured the remotest areas and the highest reaches ever committed to film. He would also use photographic techniques never attempted in those harsh conditions and at such dizzying heights before. Wet collodion plates, chemical baths and portable dark rooms were pressed into service, as were local porters who risked life and limb carrying equipment larger and more unwieldy, more unsuited to climbs, than had ever gone up steep slopes and into blizzards before. 'When the first man slipped, which with such a weight he was almost sure to do, the second was powerless, and so the box rolled down a declivity about a thousand feet. The men were carried with it for a considerable distance, causing one a broken arm, and the other the fracture of one or two ribs. It was fortunate indeed,' Bourne recounted in the *British Journal of Photography* with his usual empathy, 'that the box contained only glass instead of negatives.'

But fortunately for the photographer, as well as for the cause of photography—our modern endeavour to affix our world on celluloid—his 'mulish' porters picked themselves up and carried on. So it was in these mountains of unmatched magnificence that Bourne found himself as a photographer. He took hundreds of photographs, and when released through Bourne & Shepherd in India and Marion & Co. to the wider world, they were unlike anything the curious public had seen previously, in range or quality. And if surviving his overwhelming Himalayan experience with the help of his Indian companions had the strange effect of re-affirming his faith in an exclusionary Christian God—'It was impossible to gaze upon this tumultuous sea of mountains without being deeply affected by their majesty and awful grandeur, without an elevation of the souls' capacities, and without a silent uplifting of the heart to Him who formed such stupendous works', then the pictures he brought home had quite the opposite effect. Here were pictures the British and Indians could agree on; it enhanced the image of both and helped create that Brand India which the British would use to justify their colonial conquests internationally, and which India later picked up and promoted to boost reputation as well as trade. Samuel Bourne was amongst the first to discover how photogenic India could be, how sellable to a world now keenly interested in lands beyond their ken. He used that knowledge, alongside his technical mastery over the medium and willingness to take risks, to produce photographs that were exciting and new. Perhaps we can ascribe the continuing awe of, and the enduring need to commune with, the Himalayas, at least in part to him. And it is partly to him too we owe the global urge to grasp lands far away, through pictures or tall travel tales told by the fire. 'As the eye wandered from range to range and from summit to summit, all robed in the silent whiteness of eternal winter, it seemed as though I stood on a solitary island in the middle of some vast polar ocean . . .'

Considering his passion for the mountains, it is no surprise that one of the few other places in India that moved him to wonder was

Kashmir. 'Let the reader endeavour to imagine this lovely panorama spread around him—every object in which is faithfully mirrored in the peaceful lake, whose surface on the first day I visited it was as smooth as glass itself—and he will then be able to form some idea of the kind of scenery which delights every visitor to this celebrated valley.' Even more surprisingly he speaks glowingly (with a waspish sting in the tail in keeping with his nature) of its women. 'Many of them are certainly very pretty. Sometimes in going down the river in the evening in a closed boat, I have seen as pretty, round faces, rosy cheeks, fair skins, black eyes, and flowing locks as can be found in better civilised countries.' He was, on the whole, a man consumed by his professional purpose, and his only lapses into romanticism came in the presence of geographical beauty. That strong sense of purpose soon took him to the one place in India where he could establish himself in the manner he desired.

In British India's wealthy capital of Calcutta, he embarked on the most lucrative part of his photographic career. Calcutta was too flat, too hot, too big and too full of brown people for his liking, but he took to it more than he had to Delhi. Colonial buildings in the neoclassical style had sprung up across the city, making Bourne feel more at home, and the newly laid boulevards were wide and relatively uncluttered by natives. Those who were there were just right in number for him to feel comfortable marshalling into studied poses (or hiding away!) for his austere, nearly unpeopled photos. And so he set about taking some of the most important photos of Calcutta at the time. With many

Englishmen of his era, he appreciated the familiar in the exotic; the symmetry of the colonial city that had sprung up on the banks of an unknown river, boasting societies for like-minded men, like the old boys' clubs of England, keeping out Indians and women alike. He found himself grudgingly admiring Calcutta's Bengal Photographic Society, which appeared to have merits not possessed by those back home: 'The Society holds its meetings in the spacious rooms of the Asiatic Society. On entering I was surprised to see so many present. I was glad to find the Society in such a flourishing state; it betokens a growing interest in the art, and an extensive recognition of it in high places.' That this society, with the backing of the Viceroy of India, enthusiastically took up his work, displaying it at exhibitions, plying him with prizes, endorsed in essence that 'too technical' style of his which had been criticised in England.

Bourne saw a gold mine in setting up a photographic studio in bustling, burgeoning Calcutta, a bigger, better version of the Howard, Bourne & Shepherd Studio he'd co-owned in Simla from 1863. It was a time when British trade out of their Indian capital was booming, worth billions in today's money, and the world looked to British India for adventurous new products that could grace their homes. In such a climate, photographs of a fierce, faraway land on which the British had imposed order was just the right mix of unfamiliar and familiar for his European market. And Calcutta, he had a strong hunch, with all the access it would give him to personages and the paying public, would propel him and his studio to photographic stardom.

With portraitist Charles Shepherd, who would be the yin to Bourne's landscape-specialist-and-business-brain yang, he set up shop in a colonial building on Chowringhee in central Calcutta, where its crème de la crème congregated for business and pleasure. That the building was in the style Bourne enjoyed photographing was perhaps accidental, but that its imposing four-storeyed structure would present a facade of wealth and power to those with whom he wanted to do business was not by chance. They soon had the great and the good of British Indian society, from governor-generals to maharajas to Kipling, filing through their doors, eager to be photographed. Bourne's own 900 prints of Indian land and cityscapes were also doing brisk business at home and abroad. Within years, they were not just the biggest studio in Calcutta but had outlets all over India, and in London and Paris too. In the end, however, despite everything that Calcutta did for him and some of what he did for Calcutta and even India—in changing perceptions about them in the wider world—Bourne was eager to go home. Having made his name and fortune, he returned to Nottingham in 1870 with his English wife, to start a business in cotton imported from India. Even in leaving then, because he'd had enough, he took a piece of India with him that would continue to serve him for the rest of his life.

But did India return the conflicted feelings Samuel had for it? Well, no. Not many in India knew that he had anything to do with its international image and he remained, for the most part, a Middle English grandee. But the studio carried on after his departure, continuing to do booming business from its distinguished premises for a good while, with contracts to cover every important occasion in British India, including the opulent Delhi Durbar of 1911. And Calcutta, with its fondness for things English, its delight in its once-mighty history and for black-and-white film too, certainly held the Bourne & Shepherd Studio in high regard. The romance and glamour of a photographic studio that put a sheen on Western ideas of India and Indians appealed to this most British of Indian cities. But it was not an unalloyed love. Bourne's depiction of Indians in his photographs remained problematic. Portrayed as exotic, lethargic or vacuous, particularly in contrast to the British, who can clearly be seen as a pioneering and energetic people, these prints languished after Independence and were eventually forgotten. As was the studio, over the years. When it shut down completely in 2016, following a devastating fire a decade earlier which had wiped out much of its archives, there was an outpouring of interest and regret, but no attempt to save the studio that had outlived its time. 'I had nothing to do at the studio any more,' lamented its last owner. 'There weren't any customers I could talk to either. The world over, photography, especially artistic photography, is dying out. In the last few years, except selling of equipment and paraphernalia, there is no money in the photography business. There too people prefer to buy online where they compare prices and get it cheap. Developing and printing too does not make any business sense because people are only storing on hard drives or online.'

If mass digital-age photography did lead to the demise of Bourne and Shepherd, it could be considered a fittingly ironic end to the legacy of a man who, in never really embracing the principal subject—India— of a vast part of his work, epitomised irony in photography. Because Samuel Bourne, man of his time, colonial to an excruciating degree, was also an unwitting millennial. In his near-obsessive preference for looking at life through a camera lens, in consistently prizing the picture over the moment, he espoused the millennial philosophy 150 years in advance. Bourne undoubtedly saw the importance of photography at a personal level long before most photographers did, hence his zeal to provide prints to all the world. Specifically, individual customers all over the world, which, as he had anticipated when setting up a studio to deal with just that demand, became a trend that never died, only transmuted. In selling amazing new things rarely owned by ordinary people before, such as calling cards with the caller's image on it, Bourne & Shepherd ushered in the epoch of the ubiquitous profile photo, on everything from professional to hook-up sites. And as a man who invested more in the images of places than in the places themselves, ironically once again, he brought locations alive for thousands who would never visit them themselves.

Yet another intriguing trait marks him out as a man ahead of his time. As many modern photographers are accused of being, Bourne was a businessman and a technical wizard before he was an artist. Biographer Pauline Heathcote commends Bourne's memoirs in the *British Journal of Photography* as 'unique chronicles of photographic information relating to the wet collodion process' which he had used in the Himalayas to great effect. If his interest in emergent techniques took him far, the realism of his photos finding favour with a changing, steadily industrialised world, it also leached the romanticism out of his work. He was aloof in his own fashion; often impassive but for stirrings of patriotism, he would pine for home, feel enormous contempt for the country and people he had artistically colonised and yet energetically pursue some aspect of it that would bind him to it forever. Bourne, we know, was the very template for that, but in his amoral approach to photography, he was very much the present-day photographer. He thought nothing of manipulating images to fit his remit; planting or removing people, especially 'natives', from his frame if he thought it would make a better picture. He wasn't alone in this respect, as post-Mutiny photography almost entirely relied on stage-managing the sites of the slaughter, but he brought it back to Calcutta for more extensive use.

That then was Bourne's real legacy, born of his own detached but driven character, as well as his love and loathing for the country that propelled him to fame; it was neither the grand photographic studio in Calcutta, nor the hundreds of pictures he took of rarely visited places with a startling clarity unseen before. It wasn't even the British Indian brand as shaped by men like him; of exotica and vast wealth under rigorous European control—the jewel, so to speak, firmly fixed in the British crown. In Bourne's unintended bequest to the modern world, the shutter-happy millennial approach to how we view and process our surroundings, lies his true legacy to India and the world.

Creating the Third:
Writing, Place and Translation

SREEDEVI NAIR

What is a place? Is it the terrain, the landmark buildings, the woods, the forests, the lakes or the ponds? Is it the blazing sun, the pelting rain or the calm breeze? Is it the roads or rails? Is it the people who call it their home, their memories of it? How does one write a place? Still further, how does one translate it? What happens when places are written about or translated?

There are two obvious aspects to be considered in deliberations regarding 'Writing, Place and Translation'. The *first*, obviously, is what happens to a place when it is narrativized. The *second*, how language is used to make the narrativization of place possible. The two sections of this essay deal with these two aspects. The examples and instances are taken from *Tales of Athiranippādam,* the English translation of *Oru Desathinte Katha* (literally, *The Story of a Region*), which is the fictionalized autobiography of SK Pottekkatt, written in Malayalam—the language of the state of Kerala in the south of India. The original in Malayalam has won the *Jnanpith* Award, the highest literary honour in India, and its translation in English has won the International Translation Prize from the International Centre for Writing and Translation, University of California, Irvine.

1. WHEN PLACE GETS NARRATIVIZED

What happens to a place when it is written about or translated? Does it remain as it is or does it get transformed in the narration?

The place that is described could be (a) *one's own native land,* the land where one has lived one's life, or (b) *a foreign land* which one has visited or read about.

(1a) Native Land: When one describes one's own land, a territory of life-long familiarity, the descriptions tend to be rich and complex. Days, nights, the cool air, the mist, the morning rays of the sun, the fields, the temples, the churches—all array themselves in the narration. Such diverse images spring from a deep understanding of the land and its uniqueness which is beyond a casual or superficial acquaintance. In *Tales of Athiranippādam,* Sreedharan, the protagonist, visits several places, including the European countries of Switzerland and Germany. While in Switzerland, he meets Emma, the German girl. When she asks him simple questions about India, Sreedharan finds it difficult to give definite, unambiguous answers. Anything in India is not just this or that for him, it is also *that* and *that other* and much more. He wonders how he can explain to her the wonder that is India—his marvellous land of unity in extreme diversity! Of his country, he says:

> *In the embrace of the Bay of Bengal and the Arabian Sea, the Himalayan ranges and the peninsular tip of Kanyakumari, live a group of people who have nothing in common. As in the case of skin colour, they are different in their body structure, ritualistic beliefs, customs, languages, cuisines, dressing styles and behavioural patterns—they are called Indians!* (p. 407)

Descriptions of native land often appear poetic and beautiful, as they are in most cases daubed with emotions and sentiments. Sometimes a place is presented as dear not for anything intrinsic, but for its relation to something else, or for the associations it brings to one's mind. It is this *affective rendering* which makes the plain and ordinary appear unusual and exotic. The descriptions of native places present a blend of the real and the affective, which results in the creation of a land which is neither entirely realistic nor wholly imagined. Narrativization of place thus results in the formation of a new space, a third place.

(1b) Foreign Land: Knowledge of a foreign land is likely to be of a more limited nature, and this is generally reflected in the writing. One's introduction to a foreign land could be (1) *direct*, through one's visiting the place or (2) *indirect*, by listening to narrations, or by reading about it. The complexity of a place is too much to grapple with in course of either of these ways. As a result, the picture one gathers is likely to be partial and even prejudiced. This is so because of the *reductionism* that usually comes into play in tackling the complexity that is characteristic of any foreign place. Reductionism takes place because of four reasons.

(*i*) **Temporality:** A land is shorn of its many-facetedness, richness and complexity when one's knowledge of it is minimal, shallow or pinned to a particular point in time. The knowledge gleaned from books also can be uni-dimensional, restrictive or temporally frozen. The change of seasons, the resultant change of scene, the vagaries of climate or the intricacies of life in the place are difficult to be grasped in their totality by a visitor.

Emma, the German girl in the *Tales of Athiranippādam*, is a great admirer of India. Her father's library was full of German books on India, particularly on the Vedas and history, the Upanishads and Sanskrit drama. She developed a taste for those books very early in life and her father encouraged it. However, the beautiful pictures she had conjured up in her mind had no connection whatsoever with the real India of the present times. To her mind,

> *India was still the land of sanyasis and maharajas—people travelled on the backs of elephants—her India was the India of the Ramayana and Kalidasa!* (p. 403)

This is a plausible eventuality when one describes a land which one knows little of.

(*ii*) **Generalization**: Generalization ensues when what one sees or experiences in a particular context is taken as the one and only reality of that particular entity. For example, Emma is ready to believe that all Indians are 'sun-burnt', for Sreedharan, the one Indian she meets, is that way. But Sreedharan tells her about the range of complexions that Indians have.

> *Some of (Emma's) innocent questions unsettled Sreedharan. The skin colour issue was one such.*
>
> *The Europeans could be recognised by their white skin. The Chinese by their yellow tone . . . the Africans by their black . . . but what skin tone was characteristically Indian?*
>
> *There were Punjabis whose apple-like skin colour and sheen could put a European to shame; the yellow skin tone of the Assamese and the Bengalis could rival that of the Chinese. There were Keralites darker than Sreedharan; the complexion of Tamilians could outclass the Africans. How could this German girl be taught such things?* (pp. 406–7)

The same phenomenon is seen in the description of Indian food. To Emma, chappati is 'the' Indian food, but Sreedharan knows only too well that there's nothing that can be called *the* Indian food. He knows that Punjabis eat rotis, and Bengalis and Keralites, rice. People in central India eat both. And the dishes alongside are very different in each case. The truth, he knows very well, is that one might need a two-year course to study the cuisines of India from Kashmir to Kanyakumari.

(*iii*) **Making the Unfamiliar Familiar:** Another way to make a place less intriguing is by cutting off the edges of unfamiliarity and making it smooth and familiar by *likening the unknown to the known* and thus reducing the strangeness. The narrative mind draws parallels, and the unknown and the less comprehensible is replaced by the known and the familiar.

> *That night after dinner, he went to the park in the city. Seeing the thick, newly sprouted leaves on the short bushes lining both the sides of the street, he remembered the vellila thickets of Kerala, and the tall cedar trees with their spreading branches brought images of areca nut palms to his mind.*

What happens here is that the foreign place is not appreciated in its entirety or for itself, but is viewed as a lesser counterpart to one's own native land.

(*iv*) **Play of Imagination:** Sometimes, the play of imagination makes a land very special and exotic though this takes it far away from the real and the actual. For example, India was a paradise in Emma's imagination. She had never been out of Germany or Switzerland and had never seen India, but the very fact that Sreedharan is from India makes him perfect in her eyes. To her, he is a thing to marvel at. Though she knows him only for a week when he was visiting Switzerland, she is heartbroken when he gets ready to leave. She passionately requests him to marry her and settle down. Her imagination is so rich and the picture she has created for herself about India is so marvellous that to her mind, a person from India can only be the best among men, marrying whom would be the most wonderful thing that can happen in a girl's life. Imagination can certainly turn the mundane into the exotic, but what is described in the process may have very little relation to the real.

Thus, when places are narrativized, whether they be one's own land or foreign places, there is a transformation that takes place. The actual place has something added to it through the narrator's imagination, and something taken away from it by the narrator's limitations. The place that is finally narrated will be a *third place*—partly real, partly imagined. This is how the human mind makes something its own.

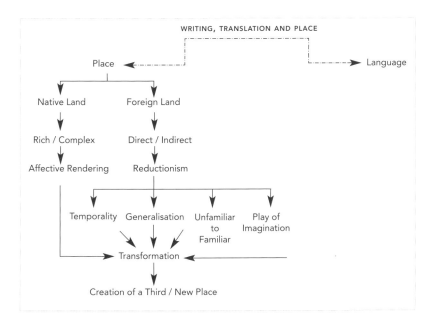

2. LANGUAGE IN THE NARRATIVIZATION OF PLACE

Anyone writing or translating into English is likely to be confronted with the question *Which English?* The 'Englishes' of today are several and they include British English, American English, Canadian English, Australian English, Irish English, Indian English, Hong Kong English and so on. However, adhering to one of the above varieties also may not make the answer to 'which English?' very specific. For example, Indian English cannot be said to be a homogenous entity. The English that is used in each of Delhi, Bengal, Bihar, Andhra, Tamil Nadu or Kerala, for instance, is distinct from its counterparts elsewhere in the country.

The English used in the translation of *Tales of Athiranippadam* is richly varied in style. There is plain, unimaginative, colourless use of the English language as in the question

'How many frog legs did Kerala export to America?' (p. 413)

However, there are other descriptions which teem with geographical indicators such as the flora and fauna of the land.

Tender leaves, blossoms and berries made the green forest look beautiful. Ripe red thetchi fruits adorned the bushes like big drops of blood and blue berries dangled all over the forest like marvellous glass marbles . . . Appu pointed to a pottikka plant in full blossom . . . he enjoyed popping the green pod of tender pottikkas against his forehead with a soft dhupp. . . . (p. 40)

There are very peculiar plays with words as in the excerpt below.

"What's Wep ran kinlew? Tell me.' [...]

'Rip van Winkle, understand?' [...]

'In a den build, rose to tower an ivory gar', what's it? [...]

Then would come the best of the lot.

'Morocco never mes two'

'Tomorrow never comes, that's it' [...] (pp. 113–14)

The conversations of no-English-knowing locals also are presented.

'We were digging trenches.'

'What's a "tirinch"?' tapper Parangodan asked.

'Kunjappu will tell you.'

'That's a ditch, a very long ditch. When bombs are dropped from the sky, the soldiers hide themselves in these deep underground trenches. Do you get it?' (pp. 20–1)

So which English is this? Should it be called Indian, and then its Kerala variety? In each version of Indian English, there are distinctions brought to bear upon the language by the characteristic features of the specific region where it is used. The English language is thus subjected to extreme violence. It is strafed to take in what is foreign to it—it is stretched, dwarfed, dilated or contracted. This process is the opposite of what occurs during colonization. What happens here is a fragmentation and a provincialization of the hegemonic English language—a transformation of the language which facilitates the containment of what is foreign. This usually happens to the language in which the writing/translation of the foreign takes place.

To make a specific note of instances when writing/translation into a foreign language turns problematic, it would be ideal to start with *names of places*. I hail from a city called Thiruvananthapuram (*Thiru-Anantha-Puram*), in Kerala. In our language, which is Malayalam, the name of the city literally means *Holy-Ananatha-City*, i.e. the holy city of Ananthan. Ananthan is the name of the serpent on which the Hindu god Vishnu reclines. Thus, by extension, 'Thiruvananthapuram' means 'the city sacred to Vishnu'. The English name of the city, however, is *Trivandrum*, which sounds slightly similar, but signifies nothing. The meaning, sound and texture of the word has changed. It now means or suggests nothing in particular. That which we call a rose may smell as sweet by any other name, but other names are not likely to evoke or induce the emotions attached to the name rose. A name bestows an identity, and perception changes according to a name. When names are arbitrarily replaced, they lose meaning, individuality, history and identity. Names in many languages, especially in the Indian languages, have meanings. So replacing them may result in mutilation and loss of meaning. Adam Jacot de Boinod, in his article titled 'What's in a Name?'[1] writes that Chicago means 'garlic place' because wild garlic named 'chicagoua' once grew abundantly in that area; that Milan simply

1 Adam Jacot de Boinod, 'What's in a Name?' *ITI Bulletin: The Journal of the Institute of Translation and Interpreting* (May–June 2017): 19.

means 'middle of the plain'. He explains how several places in London were named after hills, such as Hendon (high hill), Muswell Hill (mossy well by a hill) and Mill Hill (hill with a windmill).

Sometimes, the act of translation engineers *genetic changes* in the very structure of the words of a language. The way a word is said, perceived or analysed may become very different in the language of translation. The tone and texture of the word may also undergo considerable change. For example, there's an instance in *The Tales* where a teacher is trying hard to get his student pronounce the name Alexander correctly (pp. 354–5). He tries all possible ways but the student can only say 'Aleskander'. Finally, the teacher hits upon a brilliant plan and asks the boy to think of washermen—in Malayalam washermen are called 'alakkukar'. He advises the boy to pronounce 'alak' first and then 'sander'. The boy succeeds, as 'alak' is an everyday word for him. When the teacher meets him years later, the boy tells him that whenever he comes across the name of Alexander, the washermen appear before him. What changes here is not just the meaning but the feel of the sound, the tone, the texture and the associations. This is almost as important as a genetic change.

Thirdly, the translation of any place is likely to present *cultural markers* which could be objects or practices or events, though such words may not always find equivalents in the target language. Even if they do, the connotations could be very different. For example, *taravad* in Malayalam is usually rendered in English translations as 'joint family', but it is quite different—it is a very peculiar family setup, and also suggestive of a particular caste. This may be why many translators nowadays retain the original word if it is loaded or culturally dense. But even in that situation, its full implications are hard to convey and to understand. For example, *The Tales* begins with a registered letter sent by a nephew to his uncle, who is the head of the *taravad*. The intent of the letter is to request the uncle either to arrange his (the nephew's) marriage or to commit the money to be spent for the purpose. Whoever will think on reading the term 'joint family' that its head bears this particular responsibility? The tensions that creep into a language to accommodate new ideas and concepts make the language grow and develop. Moreover, when a particular word from another language is used repeatedly, it is possible that it might acquire accessory meanings. After repetitive use, the target language accepts the foreign words or expressions and in course of time they might create their own legacy.

Sometimes, writing or translation of places presents *new words* to a language. These foreign words that make their way into a language may not necessarily have any cultural significance and may not require to be glossed in the descriptions. They might be used by writers or translators simply because they appear to be too intimate a part of the language of a place. For example, *aiyah* and *aiyoh* are two words commonly used in Malayalam and other South Indian languages. These words have been added to the English language by the Oxford English Dictionary through its September 2016 update. *Aiyoh* is commonly used to express dismay or pain while *aiyah* is used to express derision, joy or victory, depending on the context. For instance, in *The Tales* when the fake *sanyasi* threatens to curse Gopalan and paralyse him, he cries out '*Ayyo, please don't do that*' (p. 240). *Ayyo* is just a variant spelling of *aiyoh*.

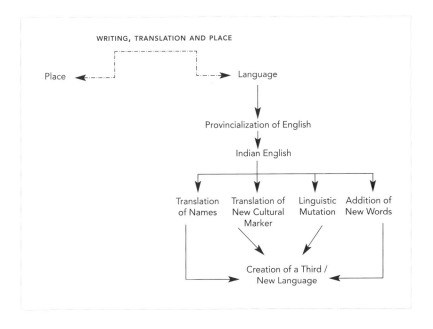

To conclude, is it possible to write places? To writers, places are often the dreams they have of them. They mix something of their imagination to what exists and create their own places. What is imagined may often have likenesses to one's own loved places. Words or images which have no connection whatsoever with the reality of such places may still conjure up, through meandering ways and oblique associations, a loved land. No place that gets written therefore is the real place. Places become a bit like some other place when someone depicts them. They become even more different in translation. A place that gets written or translated will hence be a *third place* which is partly real, partly imagined and often dearly loved!

Have You Called Your Family Today?

SARAH BOWER

Have you called your family today?

Anil lies in the centre of the double bed, feeling his sweat cool in the conditioned air. He kicks off his English brogues, which are not leather and make his feet sweat. He sits, peels off the black nylon socks and wiggles his toes. Lying back down, he unfastens his tie, unbuttons his shirt, unzips his fly and shrugs off his clothes in a series of small undulations while remaining prone in the middle of the bed. He closes his eyes and tries to focus on the place behind his forehead where the yogis say the third eye is situated. That eye, he is assured, will show him only his inner beauty and not his short arms and legs, his greying temples and incipient bald patch, the paunch that swells even when he is lying flat on his back, veiling from his view but not his consciousness, his cock. Even now it's beginning to stir, as if it has its own opinions about lying naked on a bed in the middle of the day.

The girls are everywhere. Girls tending chai kettles, girls with deft hands flipping roti or rolling ladoos. Laughing schoolgirls piled on to the back of a small truck with an effigy of Saraswati for the coming puja; Saraswati staring wide-eyed and impassive at the tarmac racing inches from her clay nose; the girls clawing breeze-blown hair away from eyes scrunched up with laughter. Girls in saris, girls in jeans. Girls with breasts as round as Mother Durga and girls with mere points of nipples pushing against T-shirts. Girls holding out grubby hands for alms, girls wearing gold on their wrists and lacquer on their nails. Their voices are in the air-conditioner's low rattle and the traffic hum from the flyover outside his window. It's the girls he sees when he closes his eyes, not the point of meditational light nor even the hot veins in his eyelids.

He will take a shower and then he will call his wife.

There is no hot water in the middle of the day, when it is expected that hotel guests will be out pursuing whatever business brought them to the city. When Anil emerges from the shower, his skin is goose-pimpled. He switches off the air-conditioner and wraps himself in the complimentary bathrobe, white towelling with the hotel's monogram embroidered on the left breast. Perhaps he will have a whisky, he thinks, feeling, for a moment, as if he has stepped into movie. But there is no ice in the minibar and his phone, black screen sleekly glinting on the side table beside the fruit bowl, reproaches him with his foolishness.

He sits in the armchair. There is a mild ache in his right hip. The unconditioned air, though still cool, is becoming clammy. Sweat springs in his groin and armpits, bringing with it the familiar odour of his body that reminds him of home. It's the spices his wife uses in her cooking, the miasma that lingers in their bedding even when freshly laundered, made up not just of him but also of her, and Pradyumna, and all the points where their three lives chafe together. He picks up the phone, puts it back down, crosses the room to switch the air-conditioner on again, picks up the phone and swipes to his starred numbers list. It's not long. The number for his home is somewhere in the middle of it.

As his finger hovers over the number, the phone starts to speak to him. *You know how it'll be. You know exactly how the conversation will go.*

—*How is business?*

—*It's OK. You know. I have a little break now between meetings so I'm calling you.*

—*And the weather? This time of year. Are you keeping warm? Eating ginger? Can you find chai with ginger?*

—*Yes, yes, I'm warm. The weather is fine. Don't worry. How is Prad?*

—*He is upset, Anil. The Kolkata train was late.*

—*It's always late.*

—*Anil, please. You know what I mean. It was late by a different time. I couldn't calm him. He . . .*

—*You must discipline the boy, Parmi. You spoil him, he's getting soft.*

—*Soft, Anil? You are never here, always on business, you have no idea. How am I to discipline him? He is fifteen. He is a head taller than me and much stronger. And the trains do not keep consistent times.*

At this point, you'll see, as if I were a window to your home, Parmi striking her temple with the heel of her hand. Her forearm is bruised, a constellation of four round, purple bruises like fingertips. How children mark their parents and the marks seep to the surface. Parmi is dark-skinned; you know she'd have taken more care to hide the bruises if she'd thought they would show.

Anil puts the phone down.

Have you re-confirmed all your appointments for tomorrow?

Anil turns the phone off. He will have that whisky, he thinks. He might even have two. Why not? The appointment book in his briefcase is empty. He has nowhere to be today, and who knows where he will be tomorrow? Pouring two miniature Johnny Walker Black Labels from the minibar into a glass, he goes back to the bed. He has brought his own whisky, it is in his briefcase, but that is for later. He turns on the TV. Flicking through the channels, he finds one showing IPL; a white-skinned boy with red hair, in the pink and purple Rising Pune Super-giant strip, knocks boundary after boundary, but Anil's attention is grabbed more by the cheerleaders celebrating his pyrotechnics than by the batting itself. His eyes rake the pixellated white teeth and kohled eyes, the gems glinting in gyrating belly buttons, and he curses the camera that only glances at the girls before swinging its attention back to the game.

He flicks channels in frustration until he finds the news. The newsreader is a woman but it's OK, she's older, she doesn't interest him. Her tone is a little strident, but monotonous enough to soothe him. He sips the whisky and feels its warmth spreading out behind his ribs. His body seems to sink deep into the mattress as his muscles relax and his eyelids droop.

Are there any important calls to be made before the day ends?

It's almost dark when he awakes, the room lit by the flicker of the TV and the yellow whip of headlamps on the flyover. A man with an immaculate silver quiff and candid eyes has replaced the woman newsreader and is speaking gravely about a battle in Syria. Coming sharply to attention, Anil discovers the whisky has spilled, soaking into the complimentary bathrobe. He sniffs the urine-coloured stain just to make sure, and his mind conjures the advertising posters he's become increasingly aware of lately, for clinics specialising in prostate surgery. Prosperous-looking couples, the men in Western business dress with hair the same colour as the newsreader's, the women young enough to flatter their husbands' virility but not so young as to question their moral rectitude.

Aware that he needs a piss, Anil gets up from the bed, peeling the sticky bathrobe from his thigh. His stream flows uninterrupted, with a

satisfying force, hitting the water in the toilet bowl with a throaty gur-
gle, and he's relieved even though he knows it's ridiculous. His prostate
is the least of his problems right now. Nonetheless, there is pleasure to
be had in the thought of a properly functioning body. Feeling lighter
of heart for a snooze and a good piss, he switches his phone back on,
resolved this time on calling home.

But there is already a voicemail from Parmi. His heart sinks in his
chest like a punctured balloon.

—Anil, you know I wouldn't trouble you while you're on business
if it wasn't important. It's Prad. (And here her voice breaks.) He's gone,
Anil, run off. He's not at the railway track. I thought that's where he'd
be. That's where he always goes, isn't it? But ... oh, Anil, where are you?
I keep trying and you never answer.

Now he notices there are six missed calls from her. Bile rises to the
back of his mouth but he swallows it down. It tastes like a mixture of
whisky and the lassi he drank for breakfast, in the hotel restaurant with
all the other businessmen and a party of American women tourists
swathed in kantha scarves, back when he believed he could get through
this day by pretending it was like any other.

He won't call Parmi, he decides. It will only make things worse.
He'll write to her, explain himself that way. That way, she can't interrupt.
He sits down at the desk, switches on the table lamp and draws a sheet
of the hotel's monogrammed notepaper into its pool of light. Picking
up the cheap ballpoint he writes,

My dear Parminder

And pauses, wondering when he last called her Parminder, and whether he should just write 'Dear Parmi' so as not to alarm her. And tells himself not to be so stupid because the very existence of a letter from her husband, as opposed to a voicemail or text message, is going to alarm her. Even before she opens the envelope.

Taking another sheet of paper from the slender sheaf in the wooden rack on the desk he writes,

Dear Parmi

Now what, he wonders, noting the cheap ballpoint has already leaked a blue stain on to the callus disfiguring the middle finger of his right hand. Where to begin?

Are there any birthday or anniversary greetings?

He and Parmi waited a long time for a child. His mother, in her element, told him this was what came of allowing his wife to go out to work. She sent Parmi to the temple and, when prayer and sacrifice did not prevail, to a herbalist who made her drink foul-smelling brews several times a day. For some months, the tang of frying spices in their home was replaced by a fetor of dank grass and drains. It permeated Parmi's skin and hair and lurked on her breath. Anil began to feel that the modern life he had been constructing for himself ever since he graduated business school was being undermined by the mysteries of his wife's womb. He loved his wife, whom he had met at college and who had wanted to marry him despite his mother, but he was overwhelmed by her biology.

Tacitly acknowledging the failure of the herbalist, his mother changed tack and sent for a wise woman from her home village who muttered spells and burned incense, which at least smelled better than the herbal teas. And, out of earshot of his mother, she drew the young couple aside to whisper that the best way to get a baby was to relax and not think about it, and that a little wine from time to time couldn't do any harm.

In due course, Parmi fell pregnant.

To begin with, she was sick. She lost weight, her skin erupted in spots and her hair grew lank. Anil felt guilty. His heart probed the imbalance in things that said a man might take his pleasure and yet do this to his wife. His mother said the sickness was a good thing, it meant the baby had taken. Anil stayed late at the office and thought about using whores. Then, as the first rainclouds of the season gathered above the maidan, sending the cricketers and goatherds running for cover, Parmi began her transformation. Like a ripening fruit, she swelled and grew golden. Her hair became thick and glossy, her breasts as firm and round as those of Rukmini dancing in the temple with Lord Krishna.

'We will call our son Pradyumna', he told her, stroking her belly along the dark line that ran, now, from navel to pubis, sensing beneath his fingers the butterfly flutter of the baby's limbs.

Much to his mother's disapproval, Anil and Parmi had planned for a hospital birth, and it was just as well because the baby's shoulder wedged against Parmi's pubic bone and she needed an emergency caesarean. While she was recovering from the anaesthetic, the midwife, masked and gowned and wearing white rubber boots, a priestess of science and modernity, placed the baby in his arms.

'You have a beautiful daughter,' she said, and the tiny, swaddled weight in his arms suddenly seemed insupportable. The midwife laughed merrily as he fumbled.

'Don't be frightened,' she said, 'babies don't break, you know. Just take a good firm grasp. Let her know she's safe with you.' She adjusted the blanket around the baby's face. 'What will you call her?'

Anil stared at the burden in his arms. Its eyes were scrunched shut, as if it were not yet ready to face the world. Its chin was well formed and its bottom lip jutted in a determined way. It could be a boy. There could have been a mistake.

Have you charged your mobile phone or laptop?

He doesn't have his charger. He knew he wouldn't be needing it.

Have you reconfirmed your airline tickets?
Please dial 2999 for travel desk assistance.

Before the conveyor belt broke down, he had stood in the queue for baggage screening outside the hotel entrance next to an air stewardess, a tall, fair woman about whom he remembers almost nothing but the patchwork of labels on her overnight bag. Dubai. Singapore. Los Angeles. Sydney. Hong Kong. Names that existed for him only as words and glossy postcard images. He has never flown, a fact which fills him now with a vague sentimental regret. He had arrived in the city on the train whose unreliable timetable causes Prad so much distress, and had travelled to the hotel by yellow taxi, careering among the tuktuks and rickshaws and bullock carts that jostled in the narrow alleys beneath the flyover, made narrower still by the streetsellers squatting among their wares, everything from onions to flower garlands, shoe brushes to saucepans. He already reeked of the city, of rancid ghee and exhaust fumes and goat shit, and yearned bodily for the cleansing atmosphere of the air-conditioned lobby. His relief, as he stepped out through the revolving door, clutching his unscreened briefcase, was palpable.

He picks up the leaking ballpoint once more, thinking he might write something to Parmi about flying, and how he would like to sit beside her in an aeroplane, sipping a cold beer and watching a movie, shoulders vibrating gently together in the hum of the jet engine. Just as he is about to put pen to paper he hears an almighty crash from the corridor outside his room, a sound like every plate in the hotel toppling off a high shelf, followed by a wail of despair. Then, oddly, complete silence. Well, he thinks, going back to his letter, someone will have gone for a broom and they will return and he will hear the sounds of clearing up. Someone's room service will be delayed, though, that's for sure.

Have you placed your wake-up call or early morning tea or coffee? Please dial 9 for the operator.

Anil considers his plans and wonders if placing a call for morning tea might make sense. After all, even if he finishes the letter to Parmi and entrusts it to the post, it will be necessary for someone to enter his room sooner or later, and why not sooner? It will make no difference to him, but perhaps it will make it easier for her. Yes, he decides, it would be a kindness to Parmi to order early morning tea. He returns to sit on the bed and picks up the room's phone. While he waits for the operator, he gazes absently at the TV screen. The silver-haired newsreader has been replaced by advertising; a girl massages cream into her face while the voiceover lists the cream's attributes. It will lighten skin, smooth out blemishes, reduce the appearance of fine lines . . . Anil finds himself studying the girl's jawline. As the screen flicks to the next ad, he realises he has been hanging on for the operator for several minutes. Annoyed, he replaces the receiver, waits a few seconds then redials.

This time the phone is answered promptly.

'I would like to order tea for tomorrow morning,' Anil says.

'Yes, sir. I'll just . . . put you through.' The operator sounds distracted, as if she is reading from a script while thinking about something else. It's not what you expect of a hotel of this class. Anil's stay here is important, and even if the hotel staff are unable to appreciate how important, for the money he is paying, they should behave as if they can. He is thinking about saying something to that effect when a man's voice comes on the line.

'Tea. Tomorrow morning. Yes.' And the line goes dead before Anil has been able to give a time. As he sits staring at the receiver, wondering whether to bother trying again, or if the gods are attempting to tell him something about his chances of early morning tea tomorrow, he hears running footsteps in the corridor. A thud. A voice. Young. Male. Pleading. Inarticulate. He's heading instinctively for the door when a burst of what sounds like machine-gun fire stops him in his tracks, one hand already extended towards the door handle. His heart crashes against his ribcage. Bright spots dance before his eyes and the patterns on the carpet, the colour of eggplant with splashes of bougainvillea, undulate sickly beneath his feet. He can't catch his breath. Is he having a heart attack? How bloody ironic.

Do you need any assistance with Wireless Internet?
Please dial 2944/333 for assistance.

The TV has stopped working. Outside the door now is silence. In the room is silence. Anil can no longer even hear the traffic on the flyover or the horns of exasperated drivers stuck in the alleys beneath it. Is he dead? Are his senses draining from him one by one, hearing gone, sight lingering, taking a last look around? This isn't how he planned it.

The letter to Parmi lies unfinished on the desk. Well, hardly started, if truth be told. No time now. He will have to call her. He will have to tell her to shut up and listen or, if he's lucky, she won't answer and he can explain himself in a voicemail. He will have to hope his voice doesn't give out before he's finished. He switches his phone back on.

Twenty per cent battery. Well, it's enough for what he has to say. The story itself isn't a long one; it's only his excuses that would have dragged it out and the one thing that is clear to him, as the TV stutters back into life and he sees wobbly footage of the facade of his own hotel on the screen, is that the gods have blessed him by making sure he has no time for excuses.

Have you taken your prescribed medicines or vitamins?

His heart steadies and his senses return to him as he takes the bottle of Glenmorangie and the packets of paracetomol out of his briefcase and sets them out on the desk. He crumples the letter to Parmi and tosses it into the bin. As he does all this, he also watches the TV. The silver-haired newsreader is back, his demeanour graver and more magisterial than ever. There is an ongoing incident at a city hotel. A number of masked gunmen stormed in just before 4 p.m. Shots were heard and it is believed some people have been killed. It is not known how many people are in the hotel although, at this time of day, most guests are likely to be out.

Anil calls his home number and waits, breathing deeply, in through the nose, out through the mouth. He is alert now, to the ringing of the phone and the newsreader's stately drone, to the tiniest sound or adjustment in the atmosphere that might mean something is happening outside his room. His own voice, sounding young and bright on his home's recorded answerphone message, settles sharply in his ear. After the beeps, as instructed, he begins:

'Parmi, there's something I have to tell you . . .' But as he pauses, searching for the right words, he becomes aware of a commotion in the corridor. Shouting, the splintering of doors being kicked down, more short bursts of gunfire. 'I love you,' he tells the answerphone. 'Both of you.'

This is it then, he thinks and, catching sight of the whisky bottle and the blister packs of pills set out on the desk, begins to laugh. He remains seated on the edge of the bed, listening as the shouting and splintering and gunfire draw closer to his own door. He could still take the pills and drink the whisky; it might make whatever is coming easier to bear. On the other hand, he could, for once, let fate take its course without meddling.

He will never tell Parmi, now, what he did. For her, he persuaded himself, but really for himself. How the midwife in the white rubber boots pulled her mask away from her mouth and down to her chin, and said to him, 'You're disappointed. You wanted a son, and they've already warned you your wife might not be able to have more children.'

His miserable nod.

Her next words: 'I have an idea. Come with me.'

How she took the baby girl from his arms and laid her in a crib in the hospital nursery, then led him to another crib on the other side of the clean, bright room. 'This boy,' she said, and they both gazed down at him, 'is not wanted. The mother is very young, a victim of rape. He was born just a few hours ago.' How money changed hands, a demeaningly small amount, and how he gathered up the baby boy and said, 'Hello, Pradmunya.'

He will never tell Parmi about the guilt which has stalked him ever since, how he is haunted by the eyes of girls and the sight of the boy, rocking on his heels in the shade of the vine trellis, his dog-eared train timetables spread across his bony knees. But never mind, he thinks, as his door splinters around its hinges and the muzzle of a machine gun probes the shattered gap, he has told her the important thing.

POETRY

Norwich Diary, May 2017

MANDAKRANTA SEN

1

Yes. Oh yes, I have been there
Where the meadows were lush green
The sky was a bright azure
Oh yes, I am sure
This is the heaven, the haven of poems,
Of which—though I forgot the names—
Only the resonance plays in my head
Like I did not write them, instead,

The words, the pauses—*they* wrote me
And I could see
In front of my eyes the poems take shape
Season after season,

                Step by step by step

2

I spoke about the Mahabharata
Kurukshetra, where the great conflict took place
I spoke about Iliad, the Battle of Troy,
Wars merciless

Every written work has a backdrop, we know
Cities and villages,
Desert and snow

Do not be amazed, don't be astonished
If I say it's the *place*

                which is the protagonist

It's not you and me
It's where we be

Writing places—oh, how to introspect

Every book has its own dialect . . .

3

This is the place to find
My story is yours, your story is mine

We belong to the same earth
Full of beauty and full of mirth
Full of joy and full of pain
Full of loss, still full of gain

This is the place to exchange thoughts
To give each other the feelings we've got

It's spontaneous though it's not easy
The weather is lovely, a little too breezy
The feelings are flying here and there
We collect them as pages—white and bare

You write my poems, I write your prose

You write *me*, says the roadside rose . . .

4

The sky told us
'I will give you my sun'
That was so marvellous
We could run, run and run

The field was ready
For our jolly footprints
The weather was heady
Smelling like mint

'Oh I want to write you'—
I told the sunshine
'Give me dazzling hues
But do not make me blind

'Cause you're so strong
I'm a daisy, small, shy
Please do not get me wrong
If I love you, and die.'

5

Come, tell me whatever you want to say
I am not here to stay
For long, that's why I long for you
O my morning's twinkling dew!

Tell me you love me,
Me, an outlandish girl
I am catching an early morning flight
So, tell me, O soft shiny pearl—

Everything, anything you say
Will suit Norwich's gorgeous May

6

I don't talk much, still you're my friends
But it happens that the friendship ends
Bonding with nature is never going to die
This is a joy of life for a girl too shy

I am an introvert, a little awkward
Who earns her living by weaving words
Earns her living! no, it's not about money
It's the river, the forest, it's the sky so sunny

They are my friends, my unshared treasure
My happiness my bliss my delight my pleasure
Do you like them, come, let's have fun
Nobody talks to me, I talk to none

Still we look at each other, as we wish to say
While the sun shines, come and make hay . . .

7

We walked along the alley
Alleys like lyrics all the way

Prose like hills and poems like a valley
We see our words gently sway

We crossed a small bridge
The river below was still asleep
It's morning with a soft sweet breeze
I loved to think the river was deep

We discovered an endless meadow
Some trees like sketches on the sky
Under which an intimate shadow
Gently calls all passers-by

I heard the call, it's hard to ignore

Call me call me call me, call me once more . . .

8

I told you what I believe
I told you how I grieve
I told you how *I* suffer
I told you how I live

You told me what you feel
Your zest and your zeal
You told me how *you* suffer
You told me how to deal

The memory still stays
For days after days
We remember each other
In our own unique ways

The time we spent
Did come to an end
As every other thing does
Those days with new friends—

Free and fervent
Free and fervent …

9

When we read out our stories
We didn't have any worries
About if it would be liked or not
Everything goes, we thought

Everything, everything is free
Like a blooming willow tree
Like a green river bank
So fluent and frank

We were lucid like this
Be it hers or his

We worshipped our muse
In the translucent dews

Do you feel what I write ?

Oh yes,
        It's love at first sight

10

I met many friends from a distant shore
I went on knocking, knocking on the doors
When they came out, I didn't know what to tell
Making friends is easy, but I miserably failed

I am well aware of my shortcomings, I am a loner
But later or sooner
I will befriend you, I know I will
I will tell you how I feel—

I know your words, I know who they are
They are close to me, not far
It's them who carry on calling from the place
Where we met, where we stood face to face

I remember every smile, I remember every frown—
Though I won't tell the names,
                          only pronouns . . .

GALLERY

In the City, a Library

PHOTOGRAPHS BY CHIRODEEP CHAUDHURI

TEXT BY JERRY PINTO

The library is an ancient human institution, an extension in brick and mortar of the brain, an expansion across time and space of the human cerebrum.

The library is a vain attempt to capture what we know when what we know is always in flux and our ways of knowing have been challenged repeatedly and variously.

The library is an elitist institution, based on the premise that the only knowledge worth having is the abstract knowledge that will allow for capture. It is not interested in non-abstractable knowledge.

The library is a dream space, a fevered dream space, a Borgesian dream of infinity. Any library with more than 40,000 books will defeat the longest human life, even if you read a book a day. This library has more than 40,000 books.

The library is a space for imagination, for daydream, for invention, for research, for investigation. The library is more than the sum of its parts.

If you need to look for what it means to be human, look no further than the nearest library. If you need to look for what it means to be inhuman, look no further than the man who burns a book.

Choose your definition.

Even as you choose, know this. That edifice which looks so imposing, those rows of books which look so welcoming, they are as susceptible to the passage of time as you are. Time ravages books just as much as silverfish, mildew and blades wielded in secret and in silence.

The book has many enemies.

So have libraries.

But the worst enemy of all is the sound of receding footsteps, as people walk away from libraries.

Tell me, when did you last go to the library?

Mrs E. G. White, *The Great Controversy Between Christ & Satan during the Christian Dispensation*

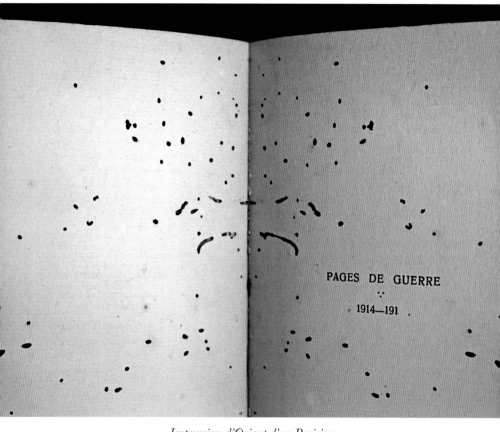

PAGES DE GUERRE

1914—191

Impression d'Orient d'un Parisien

Frederic Lees, *Romances of the French Revolution*

Elisee Reclus, *The Universal Geography with Illustrations and Maps*
(V*ol. XIII – South & East Africa*)

G.D. Oswell, *Sketches of Rulers of India*
(*Vol. III – The Governors-General and Dupleix*)

The Rev. Thomas Milner, M.A., *The Gallery of Nature: A Pictorial and Descriptive Tour Through Creation, Illustrative of the Wonders of Astronomy, Physical Geography and Geology*

Sydney Horler, *The 13th Hour*

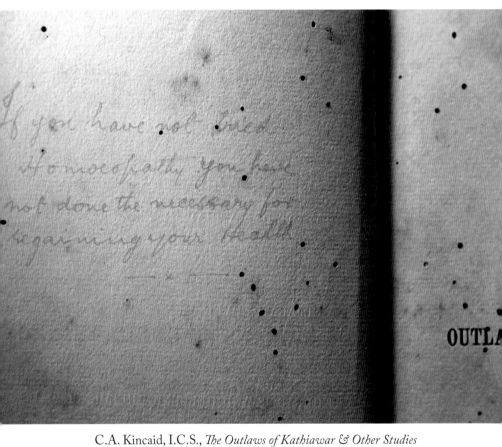

C.A. Kincaid, I.C.S., *The Outlaws of Kathiawar & Other Studies*

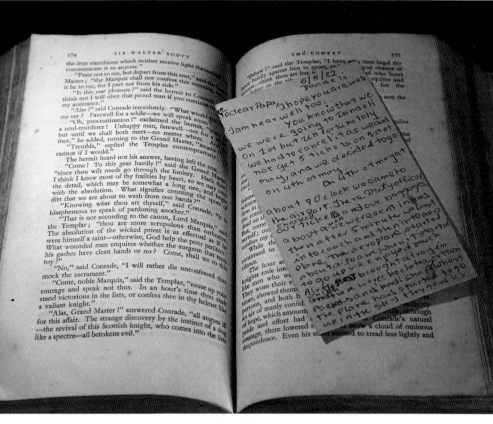

Untitled

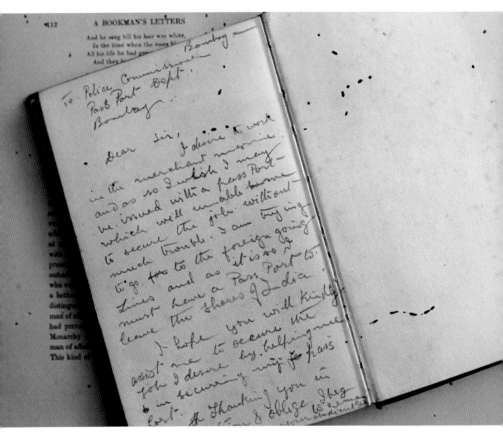

Henry Houssaye, *The Return of Napoleon*

Untitled

The Complete Works of William Shakespeare

the cow grows to a good size; those wild bulls, however, which they pride themselves so much in combating, are a very mean despicable little animal, and somewhat shaped like one of our cows, with nothing of that peculiar sternness of aspect for which our bulls are remarkable. In Barbary, and the provinces of Africa, where the ground is dry, and the pasturage short, the cows are of a very small breed, and give milk in proportion. On the contrary, in Ethiopia, they are of a prodigious bigness. The same holds in Persia and Tartary; where, in some places, they are very small, and, in others, of an amazing stature. It is thus, in almost every part of the world, this animal is found to correspond in size to the quantity of its provision.

If we examine the form of these animals, as they are found tame, in different regions, we shall find, that the breed of the urus, or those without a hump, chiefly occupies the cold and the temperate zones, and is not so much dispersed towards the south. On the contrary, the breed of the bison, or the animal with a hump, is found in all the southern parts of the world, throughout Africa, from mount Atlas to the Cape of Good Hope. In all these countries, the bison seems chiefly to prevail; where they are found to have a smooth soft hair, are very nimble of foot, and in some measure supply the want of horses. The bison breed is also more expert and docile than ours; many of them, when they carry burdens, bend their knees to take them up, or set them down: they are treated, therefore, by the natives of those countries, with a degree of tenderness and care equal to their utility; and the respect for them in India has degenerated even into blind adoration. But it is among the Hottentots where these animals are chiefly esteemed, as being more than commonly serviceable. They are their fellow-domestics, the companions of their pleasures and fatigues; the cow is at once the Hottentot's protector and servant, assists him in attending his flocks and guarding them against every invader; while the sheep are grazing, the faithful backely, as this kind of cow is called, stands or grazes beside them; still, however, attentive to the looks of its master, the backely flies round the field, herds in the sheep that are straying, obliges them to keep within proper limits, and shows no mercy to robbers, or even strangers, who attempt to plunder. But it is not the plunderers of the flock alone, but even the enemies of the nation, that these backelies are taught to combat. Every army of Hottentots is furnished with a proper herd of these, which are let loose against the enemy, when the occasion is most convenient...

serviceable, it may be supposed, is ... its reward. The backely lives in the ... tage with its master, and, by long habit ... affection for him; and in proportion ... approaches to the brute, so the brute ... attain even to some share of human ... The Hottentot and his backely thus ... assist each other; and when the latter ... to die, a new one is chosen to succeed him ... counsel of the old men of the village. ... backely is then joined with one of this ... of his own kind, from whom he learns ... becomes social and diligent, and is taken ... into human friendship and protection.

The bisons, or cows with a hump, are ... differ very much from each other in the ... parts of the world where they are found ... wild ones of this kind, as with us, are ... larger than the tame. Some have been ... some are without any; some have them ... and some raised in such a manner that ... used as weapons of annoyance or defence ... are extremely large, and others among ... such as the zebu, or Barbary cow, are very ... They are all, however, equally docile and ... when tamed; and, in general, furnished with ... fine lustrous soft hair, more beautiful than ... of our own breed; their hump is also of ... sizes, in some weighing from forty to fifty ... in others less; it is not, however, to be ... sidered as a part necessarily belonging to ... animal; and probably it might be cut away ... without much injury: it resembles a greasy ... and, as I am assured, cuts and tastes ... like a dressed udder. The bisons of ... Abyssinia, Madagascar, are of the great ... the pastures there are plentiful. Those of ... Petræa, and most parts of Africa, are small ... of the zebu or little kind. In America ... towards the north, the bison is well known. ... American bison, however, is found to be ... less than that of the ancient continent; ... is longer and thicker, its beard more ... and its hide more lustrous and soft. ... many of them brought up tame in ... however, their wild dispositions still ... tinue, for they break through all fences ... into the corn-fields, and lead the whole ... herd after them, wherever they penetrate ... breed also with the tame kinds originally ... over from Europe; and thus produce a ... culiar to that country.

From all this it appears, that ... given various names to animals in ... same, and only differing in some few ... circumstances. The wild cow and the ... animal belonging to Europe, and that ...

Oliver Goldsmith, *The Earth and Animated Nature*

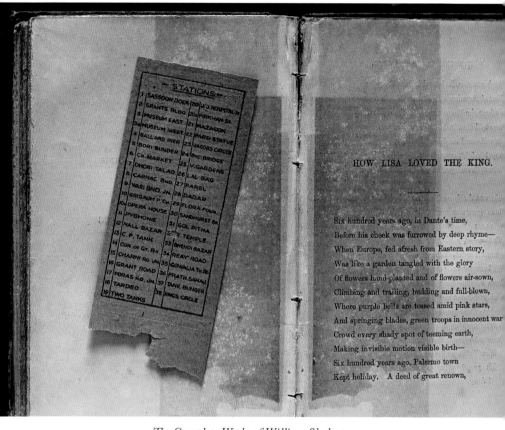

HOW LISA LOVED THE KING.

Six hundred years ago, in Dante's time,
Before his cheek was furrowed by deep rhyme—
When Europe, fed afresh from Eastern story,
Was like a garden tangled with the glory
Of flowers hand-planted and of flowers air-sown,
Climbing and trailing, budding and full-blown,
Where purple bells are tossed amid pink stars,
And springing blades, green troops in innocent war
Crowd every shady spot of teeming earth,
Making invisible motion visible birth—
Six hundred years ago, Palermo town
Kept holiday. A deed of great renown,

The Complete Works of William Shakespeare

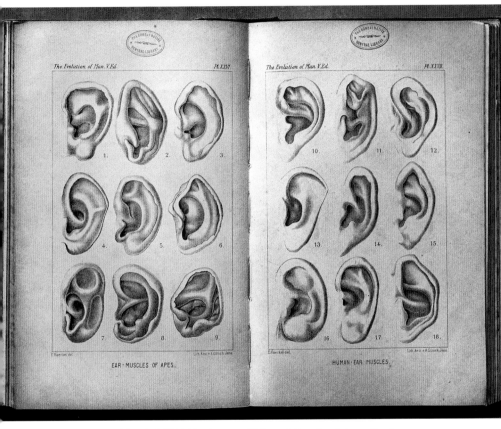

1. 2. 3.

4. 5. 6.

7. 8. 9.

10. 11. 12.

13. 14. 15.

16. 17. 18.

E. Haeckel del.　　　　Lith. Anst. v. A. Giltsch, Jena.

E. Haeckel del.　　　　Lith. Anst. v. A. Giltsch, Jena.

EAR-MUSCLES OF APES.

HUMAN-EAR MUSCLES.

Ernst Haeckel, T*he Evolution of Man: A Popular Science Study*
(*Vol. II – Human Stem-History or Phylogeny*)

Rudyard Kipling, *Kim*

The Girl from a Foreign Land

PARAMITA SATPATHY TRIPATHY

'Sidar, you are wonderful.' The voice wafted in from somewhere.

But from where? And how? Siddhartha was startled.

He opened the window. Instantly a bone-chilling December wind hurtled into the room. With it drifted in a voice, speaking in a soft British accent. 'Sidar, you are wonderful.'

Siddhartha closed the window.

A faint, familiar fragrance filled the room. Memories of the past three weeks came back to him. Vividly.

'What's this perfume called?' he had asked.

An amused smile had flashed across Sylvia's lips. 'It's called Dune.' A pause. 'Do you know what the word means to me? Vast, thick layers of sand, stretching beyond the eyes, all the way into the Sahara! Flimsy curtains of sand floating in the wind, wrapping themselves around my body. My perfume isn't just a name, it's a feeling!'

Siddhartha had marvelled at her explanation. How could someone of Sylvia's age be so mature? But then she was a student of creative writing.

It was Dr Ghosh who had prevailed on Siddhartha to let Sylvia stay in his house. His teacher, Dr Ghosh. 'You'll have to do this for me, Siddhartha,' he had insisted, 'Sylvia's father is a close friend of mine. He helped me greatly with my research when I was at the University of East Anglia. I don't have room in my house to put up a guest for three weeks. Sheela's exams are round the corner. There's no other way. Please don't refuse.'

'But she is a young woman and my wife is away. It won't be right!' Siddhartha had protested.

'Please, Siddhartha, you are my only hope. She's a UEA student doing a project on Oriental languages. Her father has put me in charge of her during her time in India. She's had a delicate upbringing, and her family is afraid that our climate and the unfamiliar food could affect her health. Please, Siddhartha, you have to help me out!' Dr Ghosh had insisted. 'Besides, Sylvia wants the experience of living in an Indian home.' He knew that Siddhartha's flat in Salt Lake had two bed-rooms. There was no way out for Siddhartha. He rang Sumona to tell her about the arrangement. She didn't sound happy.

Siddhartha and Dr Ghosh were at the airport to receive Sylvia. It was past two in the morning by the time she emerged. Siddhartha guessed correctly that the young woman walking briskly towards them, pulling a suitcase on wheels and carrying a backpack was Sylvia. She was about five feet five inches tall. Her dark golden tresses were held tightly in a ponytail that came down to her shoulders. The long journey had not left even a trace of weariness on her fresh, lively face. Siddhartha looked away. He had never liked the way Indian men stare hungrily at women from foreign countries.

'My dear girl,' Dr Ghosh took her in his arms affectionately. 'How was your flight?' he asked. She beamed at him. He introduced Siddhartha to her: 'Your host!'

'Pleased to meet you', she said and extended her hand. It was not exactly a handshake. Siddhartha's fingers touched Sylvia's lightly. Her hand was cold. The three of them drove back to Siddhartha's apartment in his car. Dr Ghosh showed Sylvia her room. It was unfortunate that Siddhartha's wife and son were not there to receive her, he told her. She was expecting their second child and had gone, along with their four-year-old son, to her parents in Asansol for the birth.

'To her parents! But why? Aren't there good hospitals in Kolkata?' Sylvia asked, looking directly at Siddhartha. The puzzlement in her eyes was reflected in her voice. Siddhartha felt embarrassed. He had not expected his English guest, whom he had only just met, to ask him such a personal question.

'They have a four-year-old son and Siddhartha thought Sumona would be looked after better by her mother,' Dr Ghosh explained. Sylvia did not say anything, but Siddhartha could see the slightly sceptical look in her eyes. How can a man who sends his pregnant wife away to her parents in some far-off place take care of a guest? He felt annoyed with Dr Ghosh. There had been no need for the explanation.

'Sir, please have dinner with us,' Siddhartha said.

'Thank you, but it's late. I must leave now. Another day, perhaps.' Dr Ghosh left.

Siddhartha had been told that Sylvia liked her food with very little oil and spices. He had boiled some chicken for her, to which he would add some butter, ground pepper and salt before heating it in the microwave oven and serving it to her.

'I'm not hungry,' said Sylvia. 'If you don't mind, I'd like just a glass of milk.'

'Of course.' Siddhartha brought her a glass of milk.

It was almost sunrise by the time she said goodnight to him and went to bed.

They met at the breakfast table at noon. The way she ate her eggs was unfamiliar to Siddhartha. She took a boiled egg with its shell intact, sliced it into two neat halves with a knife, and she scooped the egg out of each half of the shell with a spoon. Siddhartha's amused gaze followed the movement every time the spoon and its contents disappeared into the small opening between Sylvia's soft pink lips.

They fell into a routine quickly. Sylvia had to go to the National Library for her research project. Siddhartha would drop her at the library in the morning and pick her up at five in the evening. After returning home they would watch TV and chat for some time before having dinner and retiring for the night. Sylvia would tell Siddhartha about the beautiful city of Norwich, where she was born. She had a part-time job selling tickets in a theatre hall every evening, and attended classes at the university during the day. She had several amusing experiences at the theatre to talk about. People inevitably went to the theatre in stylish clothes, she said, the men often in ties and hats and the women in gloves and wraps. It was interesting to see the same people who were scantily dressed in briefs and shorts in summer dress up so elaborately for the performance.

On Sylvia's sixth day, Siddhartha asked, 'Would you like to go shopping? I'm free today and can take you if you're interested.' Sylvia was delighted with the offer. They went to New Market, which Sylvia explored with great interest.

Their car was parked across the road. On the way back, Siddhartha stepped out of the arcade with Sylvia at his heels and began walking across the crowded street. Something prompted him look behind him. He closed his eyes in fright at what he saw.

Sylvia was standing in the middle of the road, thoroughly confused. Two huge cars were rushing at her from either side, both their drivers unnerved by her sudden appearance on the road. Siddhartha ran back towards her at once, yelling 'Stop!' at the advancing cars. With a super-human effort, he swept Sylvia off the street, practically carrying her in his arms through the traffic to arrive on the opposite pavement. He looked at the rushing stream of cars with disbelieving eyes for a couple of minutes, his heart thumping.

'How could you be so careless?' he shouted at her. 'Do you realize what could have happened?' Sylvia flushed but did not say anything.

'Why don't you answer?' Siddhartha continued his tirade. 'What if one of those cars had run over you?'

'Why are you getting so upset?' she said with a feeble smile. 'At worst I would have been martyred on Indian soil,' she added, trying to sound light-hearted.

'For what act of bravery?' he demanded, still trying to control his temper.

'You could have held my hand and led me across the road instead of leaving me on my own,' she said softly and reached for his hand. Without a second thought Siddhartha clasped it tight and didn't let go of it until till they got to the car.

The incident seemed to have erased the slim line of unfamiliarity between them and brought them closer. That night, Siddhartha no longer felt ill at ease at the dining table. He had made a friend.

Sylvia was supposed to have gone sightseeing in Kolkata on her own over the next two days. She had even got tickets for a conducted tour. But Siddhartha cancelled the tickets and rescheduled his classes that he could take Sylvia around himself.

They started with Belur Math and the Ramakrishna Mission. Both the monastery and the campus of the Mission were located in beautiful natural surroundings on the bank of the Hooghly. The next stop was the Jorasanko Thakur Bari, the birth place of the renowned poet and philosopher Rabindranath Tagore. They visited the museum, the room the poet occupied when he lived there, and saw many of his belongings. Siddhartha was astonished at Sylvia's interest and enthusiasm.

After this he took Sylvia to Saint Teresa's house. 'This is the home of Mother Teresa, who's now been made a saint,' whispered Siddhartha in Sylvia's ears. 'I use the word "is" because you can feel that she is still here—at least, her essence is here.' Sylvia seemed to be in a trance. 'There are so many surprises here, so much variety,' she whispered back.

'Yes, different languages, religions, creeds, ideas, all coexisting . . .' Siddhartha was practically speaking to himself. 'Kolkata is a never-ending city. The more you explore the more remains unseen. The more you understand it, the more mysterious it seems. It's enormous, it's passionate, it's throbbing with energy. Of course, parts of it are weary too.'

'Yes, so many people, so much chaos, but it seems there is an inner rhythm,' Sylvia replied.

'You must taste our real food now. I've been giving you sanitised meals. Bengal is famous for its sweets.' Siddhartha insisted that Sylvia try some rashogolla and mishti doi.

'Delicious!' Sylvia ate with great relish.

After a break for tea they went off towards Victoria Memorial.

'Victoria Memorial is lovely in the afternoon. We'll visit the museum for a quick history of the British Empire in India and then go into the gardens. You're going to try *khurir-cha* today.'

'What on earth is that?' asked Sylvia curiously.

'It's just a small baked earthen pot, unpainted,' Siddhartha tried to explain.

Sylvia and Siddhartha spent most the time during the remaining days of her sojourn in Calcutta in each other's company. They strolled along the paths of Jadavpur University, watched a play at the Academy of Fine Arts, and drank black coffee at the Coffee House on College Street. Siddhartha told her tales from the history of Kolkata and of India, from the ancient empires to the rise and fall of the Mughal Empire and the advent of the British. He recounted India's freedom movement, especially Bengal's involvement, the events of Independence and the Partition, the Left movement in Bengal, the evolution of modern Calcutta, and a lot more.

On her part, Sylvia talked to him animatedly of the history of Norwich, starting with the early Roman settlement and the growth of the Anglo-Saxons, and going on to the story of how Norwich became the only English city to be excommunicated by the Pope following a riot between citizens and monks in 1274. She told him how Dutch and Flemish Protestants, known locally as strangers, fled to Norwich for shelter, and that their remnants are still preserved in Strangers' Hall. She spoke of the war, the damage caused by bombs, and modern-day Norwich. Her eyes sparkled when she mentioned Julian of Norwich, the first woman to write a book in English. Sylvia talked about her father too, an eminent scholar and a great admirer of Oriental culture, from whom she had inherited a fascination for the East.

'Sidar, I want to see the Taj Mahal,' she said one day. 'Daddy told me not to miss it.' There was a compelling appeal in her voice.

Sylvia could never get Siddhartha's name right. It was Sidarat in the beginning, but later she abbreviated it to a simpler Sidar, which was easier for her to pronounce.

'He's right,' Siddhartha agreed. 'You should have stayed longer. There are a lot other places in India you should be visiting."

He called up a video of the Taj Mahal on his phone. Sylvia gazed in disbelief at the majestic monument on the screen.

'What unimaginable beauty! No wonder they call it a poem in marble!' she said dreamily.

Siddhartha looked at her fondly, enjoying her rapture.

'The Mughal emperor Shah Jahan had this mausoleum built in memory of his beloved queen Mumtaz Mahal, who had died prematurely, as a symbol of their love,' Siddhartha explained. 'Consider how different the two monuments are, Victoria Memorial and Taj Mahal.

They're made from the same white marble and are similar in design, but one is a symbol of monarchy and the other is a tribute to love. Both are famous, but for entirely different reasons. Nothing can match the romance of the Taj.'

'Such a massive memorial dedicated to his wife!' Sylvia looked at Siddhartha with incredulous eyes. 'How he must have loved her!'

The sunbeams coming in through the window fell on Sylvia, framing her face in a soft glow. She was like a freshly bloomed flower. Siddhartha had to make an effort to tear his eyes away.

The drive back to Siddhartha's Salt Lake flat was unusually quiet. Siddhartha drove rather absentmindedly. Sylvia's presence beside him was like the fragrance of a subtle perfume that hung in the air but never drew attention to itself.

Later, in the silence of the winter night, Siddhartha stood at the window in the dining-room, looking through the curtains at a large pond in the distance. He could not see the water. A patch of fog, thick at the base and thinning at the top, hung over its surface. A gust of icy wind blew into the room, sending a chill through him. A feeling of loneliness made him shiver. His throat felt dry. He could not recollect when they had reached home, or what they had eaten for dinner. Sylvia occupied his entire mind, leaving no room for anything else. He felt she had been living with him for a long, long time. Neither past nor future existed for him—only the enigmatic moments of their togetherness, creating a permanent 'now', mattered. Siddhartha wanted it to last forever, realizing at the same time that it would soon be time to say goodbye. He stood at the window, face to face with the bittersweet moment of truth, looking helplessly at the world he had built before she came into his life, a world that was wavering now. He pressed his face against the window-pane, as if waging one final battle with himself in the darkness before admitting defeat. The thought that Sylvia would leave India in just three more days filled him with sadness.

'Sidar', Sylvia said softly in the darkness, touching his shoulder gently. Siddhartha recoiled. 'Don't touch me!' his voice was a feeble scream.

She drew her hand away instantly, startled by his reaction. Siddhartha turned and looked at her. Even in the darkness he could see her delicate eyes heavy with hurt.

'Please don't touch me!' Siddhartha begged. He wasn't sure if that was really what he wanted to say.

Then, before Sylvia could raise her face to look at him, Siddhartha pulled her towards himself with a force that was greater than all the compulsive urges he had ever experienced in his life. Without a word, Sylvia hid her face in his chest.

They remained indoors all through the next day. Sylvia made a chicken stew and Siddhartha got a bottle of champagne to go with it. He lit a candle on the dining table and put on some music. The mellifluous notes of Chourasia's flute rippled serenely. They sat in silence, listening to the music. The clock on the wall ticked. Siddhartha's eyes kept returning it, aware that the moments of the most beautiful period of his life were flitting away. The melancholic flute filled him with a terrible sense of loss. He made a determined effort to put it out of his mind.

'Sidar, you're just wonderful,' Sylvia said fondly. Leaving her chair, she stood behind him, winding her delicate arms around his neck and leaning forward to rest her chin on his head. Her words and her touch took Siddhartha to a place he had never believed could exist.

The day of parting dawned.

When Siddhartha entered Sylvia's room in the afternoon, he found her busy packing. Siddhartha's gifts to her were strewn on the floor and the bed, along with things she had bought. She picked them up one by one and put them in her suitcase. Pausing when Siddhartha entered, she said, 'Will you come to see me in Norwich?'

He nodded weakly.

'We'll stroll along the banks of the Wensum. It's a beautiful river, narrow enough to be confused with a creek. It is graceful like a beautiful woman who's ageing, deep, dark and intense with experience. Your Hooghly is rather wild, ravishing, always ready to overflow herself.' She stopped to look again at Siddhartha.

'I shall take you to the countryside,' she continued. 'You can see the clearest of skies overhead, covering half a hemisphere. The scent of the herbs along the walk to Hickling Broad will bewitch you. We'll take food and wine, sit on the river-bank or go for a boat ride alongside all the white-necked swans swimming fearlessly . . .'

Siddhartha felt he was about to lose a precious possession which had been with him long enough for him to believe it was his own. He had absolutely no idea when or how to retrieve it.

'Well? Will you come?' Sylvia repeated. Siddhartha did not say a word. Perhaps he could not trust his voice.

It was time to leave for the airport. Dr Ghosh arrived, asking them to hurry.

Siddhartha's unblinking eyes followed Sylvia as she walked towards the security gates. The most precious moments of his existence, cast in human form in a pair of jeans and a blue T-shirt, were going out of reach. Just before disappearing from view, Sylvia turned round and waved. He wanted to scream at the top of his voice, 'Come back Sylvia! Don't leave me,' but no words came. Sylvia vanished.

The delicate smell of her perfume lingered on. Siddhartha inhaled deeply and closed his eyes. He felt her presence everywhere. 'Sidar, you are just wonderful,' a voice seemed to whisper in his ear.

The strident ringing of the phone brought him back to earth.

He lifted the receiver unmindfully.

'Hello.'

'Weren't you home?' Sumona sounded worried. 'I've been calling for quite some time now'.

'I'd gone to the airport to see Sylvia off.'

'Who?'

'Didn't I tell you about her? The English girl whom Dr Ghosh insisted I put up in the flat.'

There was a short, pregnant pause. 'Yes, I remember. But she shouldn't have stayed there in my absence. It's not right. Why couldn't Dr Ghosh take her to his place?' There was a note of accusation in her voice.

'I know what you mean,' Siddhartha said, making an effort to sound normal. 'But Dr Ghosh insisted. You know how he is.' He tried to explain. Sumona said nothing. Siddhartha changed the subject. 'How is Pupun? And how are you? You must take care of yourself.' The undertone of guilt was unmistakable in his voice.

'I can't dismiss this so easily,' Sumona said, ignoring Siddhartha's explanation. 'I will definitely speak to Dr Ghosh about this.' He heard a faint click at the other end.

Sacred Plants

KATE GRIFFIN

I first came across the Victorian botanical artist and traveller Marianne North while wandering around Kew Gardens with a friend, when we stumbled into her gallery to seek shelter from the light autumn rain. We found ourselves in a high-ceilinged room, covered in brightly coloured oil paintings of plants and scenes from around the world, displayed geographically, from Java to Japan, Singapore to Ceylon, the US to Chile. As an artist, Marianne North was unusual for locating her botanical specimens in their natural habitat, giving her viewers a sense of place as well as showing them plants they'd never imagined existed.

Marianne North spent much of her early life as a travel companion to her widower father, the MP for Hastings, visiting Europe and the Near East. His death when she was forty left Marianne at a loose end, so she decided to travel. 'I had long had the dream of going to some tropical country to paint its peculiar vegetation on the spot in natural abundant luxuriance.' Not that she had much idea where the tropics were: 'Walter Scott or Shakespeare gave me their versions of history, and Robinson Crusoe and some other old books my ideas of geography.' Nonetheless, she spent the next twenty years travelling around the world in search of extraordinary plants and flowers.

When I visited the Marianne North Gallery for a second time, a few years later, I realized that in the interim I too had travelled to many of the places she depicts. I'd also moved to Norfolk, where Marianne spent much of her childhood at the family home in Rougham.

Marianne was fond of East Anglia: 'I was always glad to move to clean dull old Norfolk, with its endless turnip-fields and fir-plantations, pigs and partridges, and where I had the most remarkable donkey to ride. That donkey was a genius! He could open every gate in the parish; neither latch nor chain could keep him out. We called him Goblin, after the Fakenham Ghost, and he soon found me inconveniently heavy, and made riding unpleasant by taking me into ditches and under low prickly hedges, when my only chance of avoiding being torn in pieces was to lie flat on his back or roll off; pulling at his mouth was as useless as pulling at the church-tower.'

She spent most of her time roaming the Norfolk countryside, her imagination fired by a combination of landscape and literature. 'I was not sorry when I was raised to the dignity of riding a pony, on whose back I spent the chief part of my days, following my father around from field to field, tying up the pony while he was busy with his axe, and devouring Cooper's novels under the trees he had planted, till I fancied myself in the virgin forests of America.'

Marianne's curiosity about the natural world stemmed from a young age. 'Mrs Hussey's two large volumes on British fungi were my great delight one summer, and started me collecting and painting all varieties I could find at Rougham, and for about a year they were my chief hobby. One, I remember, had a most horrible smell; it came up first like a large turkey's egg, and in that state was inoffensive; and as I was very anxious to see the change, I put it under a tumbler in my bedroom window one night, and the next morning was awakened by a great crash. Behold the tumbler was broken into bits, and the fungus standing up about five inches high with a honey-combed cap, having hatched itself free of its restraining shell, and smelling most vilely. Good and bad smells are merely a matter of taste, for it soon attracted crowds of a particular kind of fly, which seemed thoroughly to enjoy themselves on it.'

Marianne was mostly self-taught. 'Governesses hardly interfered with me in those days,' she says, until 'at last some one told my mother that I was very uneducated (which was perfectly true), so I was sent to school at Norwich.' This period of education was brief, lasting only a

few months, after which the family went abroad for three years. Later, she took private classes in music and in flower painting.

By chance I discovered all three volumes of Marianne North's journals, *Recollections of a Happy Life*, in an antique shop in the Cotswolds, near my childhood home and not far from Alderley, where she ended her days. In them, she vividly describes her long journeys, the people she meets along the way and her joy at seeking out rare plants in almost inaccessible places. She gives the impression of an independent woman, by turns sociable and solitary, with little patience for those too self-absorbed to notice the natural world around them.

One of the places where our paths have crossed is Calcutta, which Marianne visited in 1878, and I visited a number of times from 2016 to 2018. There are echoes of the Bengal countryside of her time; you can still find 'whole forests of palmyra-palms' set in the water, and the raised bamboo platforms and cottages on stilts at the edge of swampy ponds covered in green algae.

In the city, Marianne stayed in a huge cosmopolitan hotel, unnamed in her journal, in a suite of great rooms 'with all sorts of curious creatures running over the floor. Six huge adjutant-birds were sitting on the top of the tall house opposite. I had seen them also on trees as I came along, which did not suit their long toes. They help themselves about with their beaks as old gentlemen help themselves with their walking-sticks.'

Marianne had a wealth of contacts around the world, either through family connections, or from meeting people on her travels.

Although she was often critical of the inward-looking nature of colonial society, she seems to have had a good time in Calcutta. 'Nearly every one was out of Calcutta, and my only friends were Mr K., the manager of Newman's (the great bookseller), and his wife, whom I had met in the steamer coming out. I could not have had kinder or more efficient friends. I met some of the most agreeable and best educated people at their house, and seldom have heard better talk.' I tried to track down Newman's, but the address in Old Court House Street turned out to be the Great Eastern Hotel, part of which is now under renovation. Neighbouring buildings have also fallen into disrepair, with banyan trees growing from the roof.

Another of Marianne's friends in Calcutta was Miss S., 'a young English lady who had undertaken the employment of teaching the wife of a Rajah of high rank, who had himself gone to see Europe. His poor little bride (a mere child) feared he would come back with a perfect contempt for all native ways, and she wished to educate herself and be taught the ways of Europe, so as not to disgust him on his return. Miss S. was a very bright, lively girl, and said it was a most amusing and interesting occupation teaching the poor little Rani, and telling her about the outer world. She even took her out sometimes (well veiled and incog.) to see sights.'

As was often the case, the focus of Marianne's stay in Calcutta was the botanical garden across the Hooghly River. I made my own pilgrimage early one morning, the streets relatively quiet, the gardens almost empty with mist rising from the ponds. In the now neglected

gardens, I could imagine Marianne searching out a quiet corner to set up her easel.

'The famous botanic gardens are six miles from Calcutta, but the whole drive is full of interest and wonderful vegetation. A German was director of the gardens in Dr King's absence, and went heart and soul into my work of hunting up the Sacred Plants. He put me into the hands of a learned baboo who said "it pleased him much that I should take so much trouble about the flowers that Siva loved," and he told me many things about them. One plant, the "Bah," a famous cure for dystentery, he said he never passed without bowing to, and always put a leaf in his pocket every morning, then nothing could happen to him,—he must be safe, as Siva loved all who were near these trees. He also told me that when he felt old age coming he should go to Benares and die there, and so be quite sure of going to heaven.

'The flowers I was in seach of were still out of bloom, so I left Calcutta again the next morning at 7.30.'

FICTION

April Fool

SIRSHO BANDYOPADHYAY

1

Delhi–London–Delhi. Departure: 31 March. Return: 7 April. British Airways. Shurjo drummed on the table in excitement after booking his ticket, overcome with joy. This was like a treasure-hunt from childhood.

The whole thing began very strangely. Shurjo was in the supermarket, lost in thought about whether to take the plain tomato sauce or the chilli-tomato, when his mother called, asking for a packet of mustard powder. As soon as he turned away from the phone, his eyes fell on the yellow tin. 'Colman's of Norwich. Mustard Powder.' But his mother flew into a rage when she saw it. 'Big mistake asking you. Here I am trying to make a fish curry, and you get this foreign mustard. Are you never going to get some sense into that head of yours?'

The cook went off grumbling to buy what Shurjo's mother needed. And Shurjo stalked off in annoyance to his room. Mustard was mustard, how could it be foreign or Indian. Unscrewing the cap, he discovered a sealed packet of mustard powder inside, folded around which was a lovely, pale violet sheet of paper. Imagining it to be a recipe, Shurjo unfolded it to get the shock of his life. A handwritten note in deep blue ink on the thin sheet of paper. 'Meet me at Colman's. I'll tell you a secret.' And below it: 'Look inside the big fruit.'

Shurjo was intrigued. Googling Colman's, the first link was to 'Colman's of Norwich'. Exactly as written on the tin. So he had to go to Norwich to learn this secret. This was exciting. His next thought was, why not go? How thrilling it would be to travel to a distant, unknown city on a whim!

What followed was what always happened when Shurjo was possessed by an idea. He had bought his Delhi–London–Delhi ticket online a few minutes go. Now for the Calcutta–Delhi–Calcutta tickets. And then, train tickets from London to Norwich and back.

Everyone who knew Shurjo was aware that this was how he did things. One night he had gone out for a paan and ended up in Darjeeling with the members of the neighbourhood trekking club, dressed in a kurta, pyjamas and slippers, with paan in his mouth. He had had to buy winter clothing in Darjeeling. Behind his back people referred to him as 'cracked'. They also considered him the entitled son of a rich man. His father was a famous doctor who had died young, leaving a fortune behind. His grandfather had amassed a great deal of property, with no one to inherit any of this besides Shurjo. Almost thirty-two now, he had not married yet. All he had by way of family was his mother. So he blew his money without a care in the world.

This was not entirely correct, however. It was true that Shurjo was extravagant, and sometimes acted on a whim, but he wasn't a bad sort. A little childish, if anything. Even at this age, he was carried away by passing fancies, just like the present one—chasing a mystery to Norwich. Shurjo rubbed his hands in excitement as he explored the British Rail websites. There were plenty of trains he could take. He would have to take the Underground from Heathrow to Liverpool Street station and change for Norwich. He even found a mobile app named Trainline to buy and download the tickets to his phone. Brilliant.

2

Getting off the train in Norwich, Shurjo looked around. The station was small but beautiful, and spanking clean, as all stations here were. But he couldn't see a fruit shop anywhere. The first clue on the slip of paper had said, 'Look inside the big fruit'. Surely he wasn't supposed to have done that in London, or was he? Shurjo frowned, thinking. There was a fruit shop at Liverpool Street station, where he had taken the train to Norwich. Or was it a florist? Oh no, he was confused now.

Shurjo stood on the platform for some time with his luggage. Suddenly he felt he had embarked on a silly misadventure. He shouldn't have waltzed off to Norwich all the way from Calcutta on the basis of a line in a slip of paper tucked into a tin of mustard powder.

Now what? What should Shurjo do? Should he go back, or should he explore Norwich now that he was here, and see if he could unravel the mystery?

A cup of tea or coffee would be ideal to unravel the knots in his head. Shurjo walked towards the exit. A cold wind blew in through the open door. It wasn't usually as chilly at this time of the year, but this year was an exception. The open fields and the grass on them he had seen through the train window seemed to have been covered by a thin white sheet. What they called frost. The violent swaying of the treetops made it obvious there was a stormy wind. Really, what sense did it make to have abandoned Calcutta's balmy spring for such cold weather?

There was a cafe just outside the exit. Shurjo entered. A young woman appeared with a smile as soon as he presented himself at the counter with his luggage. Shurjo asked for a coffee and a sandwich. She turned around to make his coffee. A shelf on the wall held glasses of various shapes and sizes, with a large pumpkin nestling among them.

Why a pumpkin? It wasn't Halloween, that was in October. As his eyes drifted towards the ceiling while he pondered, Shurjo stiffened. He hadn't realised when he entered that the cafe was named Pumpkin. His heart leapt in joy. Of course! Pumpkin! Big fruit! 'Look inside the big fruit.'

Shurjo had the slip of paper in his hand by the time the young woman turned back towards him with his coffee on a tray. Unfolding the pale violet sheet, he held it out to her. 'Perhaps you know something about this,' he said. 'I'm looking for the next clue.'

Instead of taking the piece of paper from him, she flashed a glance at it and shouted over her shoulder, 'Someone's here for the treasure-hunt, Sam.'

Shurjo had not been expecting to see the giant of a man with a bad-tempered expression who emerged from the back. The man was frowning at him suspiciously. Still Shurjo offered him the sheet of paper as affably as he could. The man did not display the slightest interest. His lips parted behind his bushy moustache, and a coarse voice matching his looks emerged. 'But he's not the right one, he's a tourist.'

He was about to disappear through the door at the back when the young woman said challengingly, 'But he's got Emma's note.'

Shurjo had no idea what was going on. What did the man mean, he was not the right one. What if he was a tourist? Had they been expecting someone else, then? In which case why had the slip of paper reached Shurjo? And who was this Emma anyway?

The man was glaring at Shurjo, examining him from tip to toe, making him squirm. Meanwhile the young woman was staring aggressively at Sam. Eventually the giant shrugged, opened a drawer, brought out a small bottle of wine and held it out to Shurjo. He didn't wait a moment after Shurjo took it, wheeling around and disappearing at the back. Shurjo turned the bottle over in his hand. It was the size of the wine bottles they served on flights, with a screwed on lid. Instead of wine, though, it held a rolled-up piece of paper, which Shurjo took out quickly.

This time the words weren't written by hand, but typed out using an old typewriter. 'Look inside the girl's head.'

Shurjo was taken aback. Who was this girl whose head he must look inside? Was it the young woman standing opposite him? And what did it mean, look inside her head? 'And where do I find this girl?' he asked the woman behind the counter.

She smiled. 'Seek and ye shall find.'

Shurjo smiled too. It was obvious she wasn't going to reveal anything more. Thanking her, Shurjo paid for his coffee and sandwiches and sauntered over to a table. All right. At least it was clearly not a hoax. But what Sam had said was worrying him. Shurjo was not the right one, he had said. Who was the right one, then? Whom were they trying to lure to Norwich with all these elaborate arrangements? It wasn't a scam, was it? But then why would the young woman at the counter smile at him? Or was Sam actually trying to do him a favour?

Never mind, he would see, decided Shurjo, finishing his sandwich and sipping his coffee. Now to find a hotel. He had made the mistake of not booking one beforehand, but then that shouldn't create too much of a problem. Emerging from the belly of the Pumpkin, Shurjo found a row of taxis waiting outside. The driver of the first one was an aged man. Shurjo went up to him and smiled. 'Good afternoon, I'm looking for a hotel.'

'What kind of hotel, sir? Do you want something modern, or would you prefer a traditional sort of place?'

Shurjo took no time answering. Modern hotels were all the same. He'd prefer a traditional one.

The driver seemed pleased by his choice. Proudly he said, 'We have one of Europe's finest heritage hotels here in Norwich, sir. The Maid's Head.'

Shurjo was startled. The Maid's Head. The slip of paper in his pocket said, 'Look inside the girl's head.'

3

Shurjo was standing foolishly outside the small shopping centre with a glass roof and patterned floor, The Royal Arcade. His treasure hunt had ended abruptly.

And yet, everything had been going perfectly so far. He had asked for the third clue while checking in at The Maid's Head. The man at the reception counter seemed a little annoyed at first before summoning a polite smile to his lips and handing him a sealed envelope. It held a card with a motif in gold. 'Go shopping! Like the king does!'

Wondering what this meant, Shurjo raised lifted his eyes from the card and noticed the pile of pamphlets at one end of the counter. 'Royal Arcade, Norwich,' said one of them.

Hurrying to the arcade, Shurjo had noticed the shop immediately. A mustard-coloured signboard with the words 'Colman's Mustard'. But it was closed.

He was looking again at the thin sheet of paper the colour of onion-skin with the words in deep blue when a young woman came out of the toy store opposite him. 'Can I help you, sir?'

Holding the sheet of paper up between his fingertips, Shurjo had asked with great excitement, 'Are you Emma?'

No, she wasn't. Emma used to work at the Colman's shop, she told him. She knew Emma well, and she knew those pale violet sheets of paper with words in dark blue ink even better. It was a game Emma used to play. She would often stuff a sheet like this inside a tin, but it was for local customers only. Just for fun. Everyone at the Pumpkin Cafe at the station and at The Maid's Head knew Emma, and they would play along. But what was funny was how one of the tins had crossed the seas to reach Calcutta. And the young woman was astonished that someone could travel all the way from India to England on the basis of such a piece of paper.

But things had taken a turn for the worse. Emma had lost her job. As had many others. The shop had closed down, and the owners of a brand, a multinational corporation, were moving the Colman's factory out of Norwich. Not everyone values history or tradition, the young woman told Shurjo sadly.

Shurjo had walked away in dejection. But suddenly he remembered something that made him want to laugh. He began to chuckle.

'What's so funny?'

Shurjo hadn't realised when the young woman from the toyshop had come up to him. She was looking at him smilingly.

'Don't forget the date,' Shurjo told her. 'First April. April Fool's Day. A day to be made a fool of. Just that it was a little expensive for me.'

Eastern Front

ANJALI JOSEPH

The first time I went to Calcutta, in December 2013, was brief—an overnight stay on my way to Assam. I was living in Norwich then, and had been for three years while doing a PhD, teaching and writing. I don't know what if anything I expected in Calcutta—it's one of the great metropolises of India, historically an important city, and yet for me it had always seemed distant. Something or other had taken me to Madras (Chennai), Delhi, Bangalore; I'd spent some childhood and some adult years in Mumbai and often visited nearby Pune, where my parents had been living for twenty years. Calcutta had never quite happened for me. The morning I was due to leave, I went for a walk down

Park Street, had a cup of coffee in Flury's, on Rosinka Chaudhuri's recommendation, and then walked further down Park Street, till I crossed Chowringhee (a name from books) and walked along by the side of a maidan. A yellow tram went by. I saw, hanging on the railings of the park, colourful pieces of cloth that were the clothes and sheets of pavement dwellers. Pavement dweller is not specific enough a term: I looked into the faces of these people, hanging out their laundry on the railings, and felt slightly embarrassed. This was where they lived now and it was I who was intruding. ('Fucking bitch,' as a lady on the wide footpath near the State Assembly in Mumbai said to me quite recently, in English, when a friend and I, walking past at ten at night, didn't get off the footpath fast enough for her liking; the pavement dwellers there were in the process of readying themselves for sleep, combing their hair, washing their feet.)

I didn't have much time that sunny winter morning. I turned back after a while and crossed Chowringhee again; walked back up Park Street towards my hotel. I hadn't realised Calcutta would delight me. I'd heard about it, read of it, at least as a backdrop in Bengali novels and stories, and in Amit Chaudhuri's book on the city, but it was still new to experience it for the first time. The city seemed to have been constructed exactly as per my aesthetics, at least visually and architecturally: a broken-down ornamented wall here, from which the sapling of a peepal tree sprouted; the dusty maidans in sun; even the anachronistic looking pedestrians on Park Street, walking along in their shirts and trousers and oblong sleeveless sweaters. They looked as people used to look before it became possible and important to wear clothing with logos on it. They looked like people who read books.

Eight months later, moved by a collection of emotions, including the sense that it was time to move on from Norwich, and a feeling of pleasure at doing the unexpected thing, I moved to Guwahati. From the ground-floor flat in a seventeenth-century Huguenot weaver's stone cottage left like a single anachronism on St George's Street, I packed up some of my books, took the rest to the various charity shops nearby on Magdalen Street, and left. I'd lived in the flat for two years, after moving in for what I thought would be a few months while I finished my PhD. I liked Norwich, and yet always wondered what I was doing there. Much of the narrative of my life had happened in big cities: Bombay, Paris, London, Bombay again. The one long exception had been eleven years growing up in a provincial town, Leamington Spa, in Warwickshire, a place for which I have almost no affection and which I more or less spent eleven years waiting to get out of. And yet those might have been formative years for a writer. I had little to do, and few friends; I didn't like school; I spent a lot of time reading, or walking around, thinking about things, writing. I left Leamington without regret. In my first week as an undergraduate in Cambridge, one of the first things at which I rejoiced was that, sitting and reading in my first-floor window overlooking Green Street in town, I could hear below on the street many voices, many accents, many languages: Spanish, French, and others. After years of what seemed like seclusion, I was back in the world.

Now, so far removed from them, I rarely think of those years in Leamington, except as an aberration, or with a kind of superstitious horror. They were not a fun time. Removed from the expansiveness and warmth of an extended family in Bombay, strange and unlovely things happened to our nuclear family when, mostly, we spent all our time together (or trying not to be together) in one Victorian brick house. My grandparents, to whom I'd been very close, died in Bombay while we were there in England. I missed sunshine, the culture and fun and cosmopolitanism of a large city. And—this was the 1980s—our friends and relatives pretty much assumed that that was that; we'd emigrated to the West and would now remain 'NRIs' or non-resident Indians.

When I was in college, my father left the University of Warwick, where he'd been teaching, and got a new job. My parents moved back to India, but to Pune, not to Bombay. A small flat remained in Leamington; my brother and I periodically stayed there for a few weeks in between other things. Now, after doing a PhD in philosophy at Warwick, my brother lives there. But Leamington was not for me. Every time I turned up—for a weekend, or for Christmas if I had no other plans—I felt depressed, as though the eleven lean years would, like the thin ears of corn in the Bible, eat up any intervening happiness, or any future possibility of happiness, and doom me to further provincial incarceration.

Spending a year in Norwich during my Master's seemed like a detour related to that experience. I lived with three friends off the Dereham Road; nearby there was a chippy that reeked of synthetic vinegar, just like the one near the house in which I'd grown up. In Norwich there were people who stared hard at me as I walked past. This was 2007, and some people on the Dereham Road even stopped, turned around, and looked longer and harder. I'm not sure they'd seen a non-white person before, except possibly on television. At the railway station I was once carrying an espresso and buying a bottle of water before getting on a London-bound train. Oh, said the lady in the shop, that's a tiny little coffee you've got isn't it? I haven't seen a cup that small before. Norwich, a bit like Leamington, had various aspects. It was a university town, and studded with cheerful hipster vegetarian cafes and solid, expensive boutiques, but it also had a core of lack of education, resentment and hopelessness. That 1980s world of corner shops and concrete shopping centres, and people who might want to beat you up just because they didn't like the way you looked, was still clearly present, maybe not so much in the University campus or the centre of town but in areas like Magdalen Street or Dereham Road.

When I was fourteen, I had a Sunday job—at the newsagent down the road from my house. At that time it was called Finlays, I think. I worked behind the till, or sometimes stacking the shelves, from seven till one. The other person on duty was usually Rose, who was probably in her forties. She'd worked in that shop, the same one, since she was sixteen. She didn't get holidays, or sick leave, and was paid every week, like me, by cash in a small square brown envelope on which the week's salary was written at the top in black ballpoint pen, along with her name. She hadn't been on a holiday in years, and never been abroad. At the time some of the tabloid newspapers were running short trips to France for a pound as a promotion. I asked Rose if she'd consider going, just to see what it was like. She said she'd think about it. She could be sharp, but she was kind. I didn't work at the shop for all that long—less than a year—and years later, Rose would ask my mother when she went to pay the newspaper bill how I was, what I was doing. The shop went through various changes of owner, but probably still exists. Rose might still work there. I'd like to think she's better paid and can take a day off if she isn't well, but I wonder. Maybe by now she's retired.

When I lived in Weaver's Cottage, on St Georges Street in Norwich, I re-entered the world of Rose, or some of the people I'd been at comprehensive school with in Leamington. The cottage itself was very nice. Right outside was the inner ringroad, and nearby Magdalen Street and the flyover under which, for a few months, I'd walk to the gym most days. In the two years I lived there, I travelled quite frequently: to South Africa, Sri Lanka, China, India, but also for a week at a time to teach a residential writing course in Oxford or Devon or Yorkshire. In between, when I was at home, the days unrolled, sometimes leisurely, but also oppressively empty. I read; I wrote; I tidied up; I cooked. There was a lot of time. Often, I felt as though the Leamington days, of never being in a hurry, never really having anywhere to be, had returned. Assuming I was still able to pay the rent, I might have continued living like this forever, or at least a long time—as though I'd moved back to Leamington and, beguiled by afternoon television, forgotten to leave.

But after a couple of years of teaching, living in Norwich, finishing my PhD, and, one snowy January, spending a week in the Van Dal shoe factory only fifteen minutes' walk from home, up a hill off Mousehold Avenue and with a view to the cathedral, there was no longer any reason to stay. I started thinking of other places I might want to live: did I want to go back to India? Not, I knew, to the Bombay where I'd spent four years working as a journalist. It was too expensive, too hectic now. Four years of living in Norwich had done something to me, besides making me revisit my provincial English past. Norwich had slowed me down, and in a good way. When I came back after a stint living in London, at first I'd been appalled by the smallness of the place, the way I trod the same streets daily and began to know the other faces whom I saw in town. Even though we'd never met, we started smiling at each other. Later, I came to value the same quality. I could have a chat to a coffee shop owner one week, go back a few weeks later, and resume the conversation; I went to readings or events and got to know friends of friends, and when we ran into each other on the street there was always time to talk. Commuting meant walking, and rarely for more than an hour. People were intelligent, and read, and listened to music and watched films. They hadn't yet filled up their quota of friends, as people in larger cities often seem to have. I made friends in an unhurried way: went out for a beer, or watched a film.

In part, it was this experience that drew me to Assam, a place where people are intelligent and lettered, but (usually) softly spoken and polite. Even in Guwahati, the capital, and one of the brasher parts of the state, people are always smiling and stopping to talk when they meet. When

I've been away and returned, people in the neighbourhood shops ask where I'd gone. The lady who sells herbs and ducks' eggs outside the riverside market knows my face, and always cheats me with a smile.

Calcutta proved to be something of a gateway to this experience for me. It is a big city, too hectic and too full of traffic and noise to be somewhere I can imagine living happily at this point. Yet I'm drawn to its beauty-in-ruins—the candy-coloured houses of Bhowanipore or Sealdah, the peaceful terraces and small lanes of Ballygunge, where you can hear a neighbour's radio or listen to his conversations. Calcutta is also trying to reinvent itself to reclaim a time when it was commercially strong as well as culturally dominant—flyovers are coming up (and, in one recent case, down), the city's street furniture has been painted blue and white, the colours of the Trinamool Congress Party led by Mamata Banerjee; in some areas traffic lights, bizarrely, emit ghostly sounding recordings of Rabindrasangeet, songs written by Tagore.

Now when I come to Calcutta it's partly as a person from the western side of India—Mumbai or Pune—but more so seeing it from farther east, from the northeast of the country. That brings its own perspective. Despite having a Bengali maternal grandfather, who lived in Bombay for most of his life, I never knew the language, but learning Assamese means I can understand more Bengali, and read the script (which is the same) without effort. Calcutta, which at first seemed a gentler, more old-fashioned place than other Indian cities I knew, now feels louder and brasher than Guwahati, but it still feels like a cousin of sorts. The further East I've moved in my extremely large country, the more it feels as though I've achieved a sense of being part of things, but also outside things—a position that's always been familiar. In Assam or other parts of the northeast, 'India' is another country, sometimes referred to as 'the mainland'. In Calcutta, India just seems a little irrelevant, as though the excitement must always be in Bengal. In some aspects, India's northeast, where I live, has things in common with Norfolk, also in the east of Britain: poor connectivity except with the capital; a sense of indignation being left out of the national discourse, but also a quiet feeling that all the real interest is right here.

Something Has Already Happened

TEXT AND IMAGES BY SARAH HICKSON

Life is played out on the streets of Kolkata. It spills over abundantly, squeezing into every crevice, straining boundaries, fraying at the edges where it is most vulnerable.

The past and the present intersect, confronting each other, jostling for position. People dance around each other on this public stage, where daily life mingles with sacred rituals, commerce, festivals and business. Everything seems to find its place amidst the drama and constant motion.

Layer upon layer, frame after frame—the narratives that unfold each day leave their mark. But over time, what was once concealed is subsequently revealed, as the layers begin to peel away. Urban infrastructure and the force of nature collide. Beauty and decay are never far apart.

My relationship with Kolkata is fragile; we've only recently become acquainted. A stranger in this city, I relish the freedom that offers— the frisson of being elsewhere, of not knowing. And of not being known.

As a photographer in Kolkata for the first time, I seek out a sense of rhythm within the frame of the city. I look for drama, engagement and emotion. I search for some definition within the hubbub; the fragment of a story, a means of containing the action.

I'm drawn to solitary figures, lost in a moment of reflection as they move through the city. I look for split seconds of connection amongst the crowds. At other times it is a sense of absence which draws me. The past and the present in conversation—a suggestion of what might have been.

Peregrine Falguni

SAMIT BASU

2024: Juvenile goes into the nest box and lies down.

It's Mrs Ganguly's first time in the Hawk and Owl observation room at the Calcutta Club and while the people gathered around the lavishly decorated dining room are no strangers to her—she's known all of them for at least three decades—she cannot suppress an involuntary shudder as she sits, as quietly as possible, in one of the elegant chairs.

What disturbs her most is how they've transformed. Especially Mr 'Egret' Bansal, usually found diving into whiskey to avoid listening to his wife discuss spiritual matters. He's at the head of the table, risen phoenix-like from his evening stupor and his eyes actually gleam as he scans the room.

After a round of updates on various prominent juveniles, it's Mrs Ganguly's turn. Ms 'Harrier' Sengupta, a formidable banker and city-society pillar, welcomes her to the inner circle, renames her Kestrel and informs the group about their new subject: Falguni Ganguly, seventeen, star student at La Martiniere, former ideal child, now displaying a regrettable lack of good judgement in her eleventh year at school.

'After she aced the NISCE I thought we were all set,' says Kestrel. 'We've always let her be her own young woman. But something's changed now. She's bored, she's restless, she's spending time with the wrong set of kids—even some below an 80 per cent SocMatch. No sports, no parties. She spends so much time locked up in her room, just quiet, saying nothing. We thought it was boyfriend trouble at first, but it's not even that as far as we can see. She just seems . . . lost.'

'You should have come to us with an observation request earlier,' says Egret. 'Someone with your social status should not have waited until the juvenile turned seventeen. I tell most of our members that the problem is not with the fledgling—it's the lack of proper parental guidance and supervision.'

Kestrel sighs. 'My mother never tasted freedom, growing up in the 60s,' she says, 'but I did. I didn't see why I shouldn't let my daughter have some too. The world is terrible enough without . . .'

'Girls of your generation often forget your freedom was an illusion,' says Harrier. 'Whatever your feelings about the last ten years, or indeed, our benevolent overlords, at least the new generation has grown up without any such aspiration. As mine did. But we are all friends here, and I did not allow you into our circle merely to chastise you. The good news is it is not too late.'

'Raptor' Roy, a grizzled army colonel most often seen trying to stay awake through patriotic musicals at the club's new megatorium, hands Kestrel a small white box. She flinches despite herself as he approaches: it's never easy to get used to his whining cybernetic arm, a legacy of the Chinese incursion in Sikkim a year ago.

In the box is a device she's seen discussed on the Net: the new Optik. It isn't supposed to be commercially available for at least two years.

'How will these help?' asks Kestrel. 'We'd not bought her any of the new smartglasses on purpose, we've seen the articles on how addictive they are. Smartphones were bad enough, and then the watches . . . we're not letting Falguni mess up her school finals with these!'

'I guess you're not among those parents who keeps cameras in their child's room,' sighs Egret.

'Of course not,' says Kestrel, horrified.

'A pity, because then things would never have come to this pass,' says Harrier. 'These are no ordinary Optiks, they're from our friends at the Hawk and Owl. You'll see everything she sees.'

'It feels wrong to do this to my own child.'

'It's for her own good,' says Egret. 'It's what every parent has wanted since the beginning of time.'

'It's a huge violation of her trust.'

'Yes. What are you going to do?'

2025: Female drifting high above the spire to the East.

'I don't know if I can ever thank you enough,' says Kestrel.

Egret waves away her compliments with a gentle smile.

'We were all very impressed at how Peregrine has improved,' he says. 'A national school debate win is no small victory. I hope she's considering a career in one of the Yogitech corporations—I might even put in a good word with my friends on the board.'

'A year ago, I would have said that wasn't possible,' says Kestrel. 'But now, you know, I'm beginning to dream. I was dreading an argument when I told her it was time to stop all the extra-curriculars and focus on her VSFEs, but you know, she just did it on her own!'

Raptor snorts approvingly. 'I'm glad to see all your worries about the Optiks have disappeared,' he says. 'We were concerned because, you see my dear, the parents have to self-discipline before the child can fly.'

'I know what you mean,' says Kestrel. 'And I have to tell you, when I reached breeding age I was far more difficult. No one knew the kind of nonsense I was reading, all the forbidden things I was seeing on the internet. I'd actually thought she'd be experiencing all kinds of . . . you know, adult stuff... but for all the acting up she was doing, her life is actually quite tame. I mean, there's a healthy interest in . . . you know . . . but I confess I was much worse at her age.'

Ms 'Goshawk Goswami', a much-celebrated astrologer-diplomat, pats Kestrel gently on the shoulder. 'We're very proud of you,' she says. 'Especially for the mature way in which you handled Peregrine's boyfriends.'

Kestrel stares at her blankly. 'I hadn't said anything about her boyfriends.'

'Which means you must have handled them well, does it not?' counters Goshawk, but the damage has been done.

'We were going to tell you today, but Goshawk has already done the honours,' says Egret with a rueful smile. 'We have been monitoring Peregrine separately, of course. This last year has been as much a test of you as it has been of her.'

'You watched my daughter have her first sexual experiences. All of you.'

'Not all of us, my dear, and don't be ridiculous, you have no idea what we've seen,' says Harrier, in the icy voice that had quelled a dozen government attempts to privatise her bank. 'And before you ask, it wasn't just us. Peregrine was one of chosen test cases for the Global Nest of the Hawk and Owl, and we simply did not have the option of letting you know. It would have ruined the experiment, you understand.

But you'll be happy to learn that she was one of the most popular livestreams among our nests around the world, and this is very good news for her career.

'Now, to business. What we've noticed among all our test cases over this year is that while the Optiks are very useful in terms of observing what our subjects experience, they don't allow us the ability to intervene directly in situations of active emergency, or help us guide our subjects towards the flight-paths that suit them best.'

'You've . . . invented an Optiks upgrade that allows you to control the wearer directly?' asks Kestrel, her voice shaking.

'Not yet,' says Egret. 'But Peregrine is off to college next year, is she not? Given her study patterns, her audience worldwide is expecting extraordinary results, but don't let that stress you out. We should have good news for you soon.'

2026: Juvenile on the rear of the spire eating. Male went into nest box.

'I'm really not sure about the smart tattoos,' says Kestrel, interrupting Osprey's monologue about the challenges of emotion-detecting face-ware.

'Patience, Kestrel, discussing Peregrine's progress is central to our agenda as you know,' says Harrier. 'And I think we're done with other business. Let's talk about our prize fledgling. We're worried that she might be aware that her Optiks feed is compromised.'

'I've asked her several times why she keeps taking off the glasses.' Kestrel glares around the room but the Hawk and Owl society is as inscrutable as usual. 'She says they're really unfashionable in college and everyone is worried about hacking. Especially after all the news out of Moscow. And in case you're planning to switch to the eyeball-attachment lenses, please don't, I've read they're not safe.'

'No, they're not: when they are, we'll be the first to have them. And you're right about the security issues of Optiks nowadays, she's smart to have made this judgement. This is unsurprising, given the intelligence she has displayed in every other aspect of her life,' says Harrier. 'It's just that she's built such a following, including so many genuine InfluRoyals, and they miss her. We've been able to use street-level and drone cams to fill in most of the gaps. But it's just not the same as her own point of view, you know?'

'I do know,' says Kestrel. 'But I also remember how obsessive I was about privacy when I was in college. Can you believe we still had paper diaries then?'

'We all remember paper, Kestrel. You're among the youngest here. Speaking of college, we do think the Diplomacy-AI-Cybersec Triple-Spec was optimal. But are you able to keep any kind of check on the paper books she's reading? Our North American friends are curious to know if she's consuming more fiction after the ban.'

'Don't they have enough to worry about?'

'Hah, yes. Can you believe they actually wanted Peregrine to transfer to New York as a student, as if that were still a possibility at either end of the journey.'

'I can't even imagine being that far away from her. You know, when she started taking off her glasses and I didn't know where she was? I've never been through anything that terrifying. That vibration when she enters my one-kilometre radius is the deepest addiction I've ever known. How our parents managed to survive their anxieties when we were kids and they had no idea where we were . . .'

'You don't know where she is? How is that possible? The smart tattoos should be sending . . .'

'No, of course they are, I was talking about the time before you installed them. And this was just in her first college term, she could have been anywhere! I knew she wasn't the type to go to protests or concerts. And she has a separate RiotAlert implanted on her earlobe, that's compulsory now. But who knows, right?'

'Indeed.'

'The one thing that concerns me as a bioparent is the sheer quantity of optimizing chemicals the tattoos are pumping into her.'

'Stop reading conspiracy theories on the internet, Kestrel. The doses are optimized by extremely advanced algorithms.'

'I know I'm very lucky to be part of this grand experiment, but I worry about her going into her twenties with no knowledge of extreme emotions and how to handle them.'

'Why should you worry about that any more than you would about smallpox or TB, Kestrel? We're hardly likely to take her off her stabilizers . . . unless you're planning to abandon the Hawk and Owl. Are you?'

'Of course not. I just grew up without these meds and so . . .'

'You once ran away with an unsuitable boy, if I remember.'

'Yes. And I'm glad Falguni will never do that.'

'Well, then.'

'I'm also very grateful for the new boyfriend. I was a bit worried about a non-Bengali family but the Sim-Baby is so gorgeous. He's a bit short, too, but I hear that won't be a problem.'

'We matched him to you as well as her. It's quite basic nowadays. And New Shanghai is a smart investment for her thirties. We can only imagine the other bioenhancements that will exist by the time their real child is born—and obviously Peregrine will have the best of what's available anywhere in the world.'

'And I don't want to sound like a Typical Indian Mom but I'm so pleased the new boy has refused to have sex before they're married.'

2027: Juvenile back up on the edge of box screeching at male.

Discussion about Falguni's second year in college is difficult because the only thing that was definitely sub-optimal about it was that very dramatic break-up, and no one at the Hawk and Owl wants to admit that there was a security breach that led to said break-up being broadcast live to an audience of millions. It is not clear why Falguni's Optiks were on at the time, or why the boy was naked and running around the room waving his arms about, or which of the Hawk and Owl's nests around the world was responsible for the leak. The official story in the observation room is that a senior Hawk and Owl member in Seoul had gone rogue and become a hacker. Fortunately the whole incident has been blocked on the Calcutta internet, and the rest of the world will be quick enough to forget, given the non-stop cataclysm that is the daily news wherever you are.

Kestrel has never seen the Hawk and Owl's Calcutta branch look collectively shamefaced before. It is an experience she finds both wholly enjoyable and utterly embarrassing, though fortunately her newly installed smart tattoos prevent her from suffering the adverse effects of either of these emotions. Her deepest regret is actually the loss of the SimBaby but there will be other boyfriends, better ones, with even cuter digi-spawn.

There are more direct issues. She wants to ask why none of the bliss-inducing chemicals Falguni was pumped full of after she discovered Zhang Long's many betrayals were enough to keep her from weeping bitterly. She wants to know why, after fifteen tearless months, Falguni was unable to speak through her sobs for three whole days. Was that also the result of some kind of hack, or other malfunction?

'Peregrine is fine, Kestrel,' Harrier assures her. 'It was just a temporary glitch, and now she's absolutely back on track. And I have to say that interlude, however unpleasant, was fantastic for the ratings.'

'What ratings?'

'Peregrine's storyline is currently the leading interestfeed in Hawk and Owl observation rooms worldwide. You have no idea how much concern the whole sorry affair generated globally, and how many early job offers we've turned down on your behalf. We must tell you, though, that you need never worry about her career again.'

Kestrel wants to express relief and gratitude, but it seems slightly inappropriate because the conversation has moved on to Osprey's tragic death. He had been so sure that the cure to mortality would be discovered before his own demise, so eager to volunteer for every new form of voluntary organ replacement, so shattered when his wife died a few months ago, so reckless in his drinking.

It is all very sad, but only good things lie ahead for Peregrine, they assure her. She means a lot to so many people, and they're all looking out for her. There's even talk of a cryptocurrency fund she'll have access to on her twenty-first birthday, a nest egg from her many well-wishers. The moment she learns of her good fortune will be remembered forever by her loyal audience.

Kestrel considers asking them about other disturbing news: about the sealing off of national internets around the world, the rumours of war and genocide so carefully concealed both at home and far away. If anyone knows the answers to her questions it is the fine folk of the Hawk and Owl, but it seems impolite to ask. She notices Raptor is absent. She's heard rumours his son was caught eating beef somewhere in north India. It's best not to spread such rumours.

2028: Juvenile heads West.

Where did it all go wrong?

This is the question Kestrel keeps asking herself, sometimes out loud. Very loud right now, and the elders of the Hawk and Owl observation room have no answer.

'This was the planned outcome of the experiment all along,' says Harrier, but without conviction. For the first time, she cannot meet Kestrel's eyes.

Had they been this useless all along? Had they ever, through all their watching, really seen anything? Had they been, through it all, just another cluster of mock-worthy old folks sitting in an old club in an old city gossiping about Kids These Days while they waited to die? Kestrel doesn't know.

Here is the only thing she knows: Falguni is gone. Flown the nest, taken to the skies. Her Optiks have been found, smashed, in a dustbin at Istanbul airport. Her smart tattoo? Peregrine has found—built? programmed? bought?—a way to outsmart it. It places her everywhere: Morocco, Hawaii, Kuala Lumpur. She's found new tech, secret tech, bought with the Hawk and Owl's cryptofunds to confound all eyes, human and AI. Face-distorting fields, biometric duplicators, emotion-reader simulators. Had she built them in college? Had hackers and cyberterrorists built them for her? Who had been watching her all these years? What had they planned? When had they made contact, and how?

It doesn't matter. She is alive. There is a handwritten note. She loves her mother. She'll be back one day, she said.

The Hawk and Owl cannot find her. Even worse, they seem to be falling apart into bickering factions. The Calcutta Club nest needs to decide whether to align itself with New Shanghai or New Delhi, neither of which option is pleasing.

Raptor thinks she has fled to join one of the neo-Luddite disconnection cults. Goshawk claims she has gone to study further, some completely useless field like Creative Writing. In Norfolk, of all places—Kestrel didn't know where that was, but is pleased to find it's nowhere near either the Welsh rebels or the advancing Scots army. If she's even there. She's too quick, too smart, for any of these old fogies.

Kestrel misses her smell most, misses the mess, the awkwardness. All those years, she knew. Knew she was being watched, planned her escape, her revenge.

Kestrel cannot tell the Hawk and Owl this, but she is very, very proud.

Translation, Space and Place

DUNCAN LARGE

INTRODUCTION: TRANSLATION AND SPACE

Translation has always been conceived in spatial terms. After all, the very notion of 'trans-lation' is itself a spatial metaphor ('carrying-across'), and so many of the common metaphors for the act of translation involve spatial practices, beginning with the biblical 'Babel' as a metaphor for the birthplace of translation itself. Introducing the King James Version of the English Bible to its readers in 1611, Miles Smith famously reaches for a series of concrete, spatial metaphors to describe translation:

Translation it is that openeth the window, to let in the light; that breaketh the shell, that we may eat the kernel; that putteth aside the curtain, that we may look into the most Holy place; that removeth the cover of the well, that we may come by the water (Lefevere 1992: 72).

Two centuries later, Friedrich Schleiermacher is speaking 'On the Different Methods of Translating' in an 1813 lecture to the Berlin Academy of Sciences, and again the act of translation is imagined, at least, in highly spatial terms:

Either the translator leaves the writer in peace as much as possible and moves the reader toward him; or he leaves the reader in peace as much as possible and moves the writer toward him (Schleiermacher 2012: 49).

Where translations have been figured as moving meaning across (*trans*, sideways), power relations between language pairs (Greek vs Latin; Latin vs vernaculars) have traditionally been conceived topographically in vertical, hierarchical terms, as have relations between translators and their source text authors (*sub*servience, *sub*jugation). Contemporary translation theory continues to frame translation—and the discipline of translation studies itself—in spatial terms, from James Holmes and Gideon Toury's map of translation studies (cf. Munday 2001: 16) to Lawrence Venuti on *The Translator's Invisibility* (Venuti 1995), the John Benjamins journal *Translation Spaces* (since 2012) and Emily Apter on *The Translation Zone* (Apter 2006).

There has been much talk of a 'spatial turn' in humanities disciplines more generally since as early as the 1980s, and translation studies has certainly played its part in this trend. Introducing a special issue of *Translation Studies* ('Global Landscapes of Translation'), guest editors Angela Kershaw and Gabriela Saldanha argue: 'The notion of space has acquired a new relevance in translation studies' (2013). What they mean by this, though, is that the old spatial metaphors—the transfer metaphor itself, plus other spatial, topographical metaphors of containment, field, flow, force, source and target, wave etc.—are being superseded by new metaphors such as landscape, in other words metaphors of 'geographical spaces', or place. For space and place are rather different concepts: place is space that has been invested with human meanings. In his classic work of human geography *Space and Place: The Perspective of Experience*, Yi-Fu Tuan remarks:

> *What begins as undifferentiated space becomes place as we get to know it better and endow it with value* (1977: 6).

Likewise, Tim Cresswell defines 'Place' in the *International Encyclopedia of Human Geography* thus:

> *What experience does is transform a scientific notion of space into a relatively lived and meaningful notion of place* (2009: 171).

I think one could easily substitute 'writing' for 'experience' in this passage, for writers so often draw inspiration from particular places and strive in turn to conjure up specific spaces for their readers to enjoy. In this essay, though, I want to focus on the kind of writing that is translation, and examine how translation relates to place. I think we can interpret it in two broad senses: a first sense which draws attention to where translation itself takes place, and a second which relates to the material that is being translated, the translation of place itself.

The first sense of the relation of translation to place can be subdivided into three kinds: (a) where the production of translations takes place; (b) where the inscription, publication and sale of translations takes place; (c) where the consumption and reception of translations takes place.

(1a) Places of Production

In principle translation can take place anywhere, but in practice there have always been privileged places of translation production—what one might call (on the model of the 'lieu de mémoire') *lieux de traduction*. As Sherry Simon puts it: 'Interlingual exchange is anchored in specific sites, spaces which enable the work of translation' (2018: 97). Contemporary translation theory is drawing attention to just how much cities are places of translation—'metrolingual' translation zones (Pennycook and Otsuji 2015)—but historically this has applied to some cities more than others, which have become synonymous with translation at certain times in their history 'translatoria' such as the 'House of Wisdom' in medieval Baghdad or the School of Translators in medieval Toledo).

For many translation agencies today, 'in-house' translation means exactly that, and it is the 'premise' of translation centres such as the British Centre for Literary Translation at the University of East Anglia in Norwich or the rest of the European RECIT network of translator houses that they provide premises that promote the production of translations, through the availability not only of IT facilities and study spaces but of libraries with concentrations of reference works and previously translated materials. Residency programmes encourage translators to travel to places that are significant for the work they are translating so that they can benefit from the *genius loci* and be inspired by their (linguistic, cultural, natural) environment. Translators usually work alone, but translation workshops and summer schools provide real-world forums for translators to collaborate and benefit from each other's company. Much translation these days is notoriously placeless in that it 'takes place' online—i.e. the translator may be working on a laptop computer anywhere they can get a decent WiFi signal, and relying on reference resources which are entirely online, or even collaborating remotely with other translators and editors/teachers/assessors, as in Translators Lab (translatorslab.org.uk), pioneered by National Centre for Writing in collaborations with Select Centre Singapore and Jadavpur University in Kolkata. But in an age of the digital and the virtual (cf. Cronin 2013), places of translation draw attention to the materiality of (the act of) translation; they are also places where translations are potentially stored in translator archives.

The logical extension of the importance of place to translation is that we should date and place translations in the same way that Joyce ends *Ulysses* with 'Trieste–Zurich–Paris 1914–1921'. If place is such an important influence on a translation then we ought also to be able to judge merely from a translation's style where it was translated. Mona Baker devotes half of her *Routledge Encyclopedia of Translation Studies* to thirty-one different translation traditions distinguished geographically and ordered alphabetically, from 'African tradition' to 'Turkish tradition' (Baker 1998; cf. Lefevere 1977; Hung and Wakabayashi 2005), and though this is little more than a convenient geographical way of cutting up the cake of translation history, in many cases distinctive geographically-dependent translation styles are discernible. Lawrence Venuti argues that John Denham's translation of Virgil in seventeenth-century England exhibits a relatively free translation style which he had adopted in the 1640s while he was exiled in France during the English Civil War, but which—ironically, since it was characterised by an extreme form of what Venuti terms 'domestication'—ultimately became domesticated itself and laid down the basis for a fluent style which Venuti argues is characteristically Anglo-American (1995: 48–51). Anthony Pym counters that such fluency is a truly global style and not historically or geographically (hence politically) determined (1996).

Translation has a default tendency to erase differences between source texts anyway, and the translator has to resist the temptation to translate all materials in the same style, dismissively characterised by Gayatri Chakravorty Spivak thus: 'All the literature of the Third World gets translated into a sort of with-it translatese, so that the literature by a woman in Palestine begins to resemble, in the feel of its prose, something by a man in Taiwan' (2012: 315). In an age of globalization it may well be the case that national translation styles have been eroded—just as the globalization of major symphony orchestras has led to a homogenization of orchestral sound (Tolanski 2003: 126–7). Some national differences are nonetheless still discernible. For example, reactions in South Korean mainstream and social media against Deborah Smith's relatively free translation style in her Man Booker Prize–winning version of Han Kang's *The Vegetarian* (Armitstead 2018; Fan 2018) suggest that Korean translation style is generally quite conservative. Beyond the situation and translation style of the individual translator, we must acknowledge that place determines the context of translation production in more intangible, higher-order ways, too, relating to what systems theory calls the literary systems in which translators find themselves caught up (how translators are trained, how translations are commissioned, how they are edited, etc.), and which can differ markedly from one place to another.

(1b) Places of Inscription, Publication and Sale

Once translations have been produced they are nowadays usually published in their own right, as books, in magazines or online, but other forms of publication have been and are still possible. For example, the oldest extant translation of the Gospels into English takes place in the tenth century in the form of Old English word-for-word glosses interpolated by Aldred, Provost of Chester-le-Street, between the lines of manuscript Latin in the codex of the Lindisfarne Gospels. It is one of the accepted norms of translation that, as a rule, a translation can be expected to be longer and take up more space than the original. Bilingual editions place the original and translation side-by-side—or, in the case of multilingual editions such as the Complutensian Polyglot Bible (1517)—the original and several translations, and modern websites such as Bible Hub (biblehub.com) or Bible Gateway (biblegateway.com) take this practice to extremes, the latter currently boasting '219 online Bibles in 72 languages' which can be consulted simultaneously. Contemporary resources allow the experimental placement of translations using forms of hypertextual or palimpsestual presentation, whereby translations can be allowed to occlude and efface originals (Rose 2018). In the agonistic relation between translation and original, the former has generally sought to take the latter's place, although translations are, of course, themselves always vulnerable to displacement by retranslations, where one translation takes the place of another (metaphorically, but also in reality, on the bookshop and library shelf). The place of translations in bookshops, finally, is also evolving, and—in the UK, at least, where translated fiction is currently enjoying a period of relative popularity—many bookshops and libraries nowadays have separate displays for translated works.

(1c) Places of Consumption and Reception

Different national and linguistic cultures vary markedly in their receptivity to translations, and the same culture can vary markedly over time: for example, the Anglo-American book market, which for a long time was notoriously unreceptive to translations, has begun to pay them more attention in recent years, and translations have begun to edge higher than their historically abysmal norm of a 3 per cent market share, even if they are still outperformed by most other translation cultures. A recent social media campaign to 'name the translator' in the UK seeks to overcome the translator's (now proverbial) invisibility, but in some cultures such as Japan, for over a century now translators have achieved significant levels of visibility and indeed celebrity (Akashi 2018). Translation theory has itself become globalized, and the works of leading English-language translation theorists such as Susan Bassnett or Lawrence Venuti are rapidly translated into many other languages so that they are as likely to be cited by a Chinese scholar nowadays as by an American. There have undoubtedly been national styles of translation theory, too—such as the Brazilian 'cannibalist' movement, Canadian feminists, the 'manipulation school' in the Low Countries, Israeli systems theorists or Bengali and Irish postcolonialists (see Munday 2001)—and counter-globalizing tendencies in translation theory have also led to the retrospective canonisation of historical traditions, such as Chinese translation theory (Cheung 2006; Cheung and Neather 2017) and Indian translation theory (Chandran and Mathur 2014).

TRANSLATION OF PLACE

My second sense of the relation between translation and place involves translating material that itself expresses place. I mentioned above that we are experiencing a 'spatial turn' in translation studies at the moment, driven by the work of theorists such as Michael Cronin (1996, 2000, 2003, 2006) and Sherry Simon (2012, 2016, 2018). Indeed, the trend for focusing in on specific spaces as loci of translation has led to a spate of books devoted to translating specific places ('Translating X') which so far encompasses America (Camboni et al. 2011; Conolly-Smith 2004), Asia (Chew 2015), Canada (von Flotow and Nischik 2007), China (Luo and He 2009), India (Albertazzi 1993; Kothari 2003), Ireland (Cronin 1996), Israel (Mintz 2001), Italy (Sciarrino 2005), Latin America (Luis and Rodríguez-Luis 1991), Rome (Graves 2010) and the West (Howland 2002). Much of the work that is going on at the moment into translating cities relates to translating the multilingual reality of the modern urban metropolis. Mostly these studies have a more sociological/political focus and do not relate specifically to translating the writing of place, so it is on that that I want to focus in this final section. To borrow categories from J. C. Catford (1965), the attendant difficulties are both linguistic and cultural in nature (and the two are related).

Language and place are inextricably linked—place is enshrined in language—and large multilingual countries such as India offer a great wealth of languages to translate from, into and between. In his play *Translations*, Brian Friel dramatises the problematic translation of resonant place-names imposed on a rural Irish-speaking population by English colonizers, demonstrating that—even with material that is often claimed to be untranslatable—where there's a will (to impose by force) there's a way (1981; cf. Italiano 2016). Even within individual languages, though, there are major questions for the intralingual translator relating to linguistic varieties and the translation of the geographically determined, place-affected language that is dialect (cf. Epstein 2012; Rosa 2012). Specifically, how should a translator render dialect speech (or narration) in such a way as not to normalise it but to achieve an equivalent (linguistically 'marked') effect on the reader of the target language as the source-text author achieved on the reader of the original? Many strategies have been proposed, but it is a notorious shibboleth and represents one of the areas where translators are most likely to feel dissatisfied with their solution.

Dialect is an extreme way in which the language of the original text conveys a sense of place, but all texts do this to a greater or lesser extent, including those written in standard language. Writers conjure up a sense of place through various kinds of topical-cultural reference (which resist translation), and again the question is how to translate (or not translate) these appropriately. Susan Bassnett quotes Robert Adams arguing that there is a limit to how far the translator can go with substitutions for proper names and other cultural terms: 'Paris cannot be London or New York, it must be Paris; our hero must be Pierre, not Peter; he must drink an aperitif, not a cocktail; smoke Gauloises, not Kents; and walk down the rue du Bac, not Back Street' (2002: 123). Such an injunction (originally in Adams 1973: 12) doubtless strikes the contemporary reader as overly prescriptive, though, for not only have films routinely adapted screenplays to 'local' (American) expectations—for example, by turning Wim Wenders' Berlin-based *Wings of Desire* (Der Himmel über Berlin,

1987) into Brad Silberling's LA-based *City of Angels* (1998)—but more experimental literary translations (especially of drama) routinely do this, too. Bassnett's own solution here is to recommend that the translator always seek a functional equivalence, but we know from Eugene Nida's similar recommendation to Bible translators—that they should seek a 'dynamic equivalence' which might have an 'equivalent effect' on the target-language readership—that such innocuous-sounding recommendations can hide significant ideological traps. In tailoring a translation to suit the target readership, dynamic equivalence is often characterised by significant shifts away from semantic equivalence to the source text—for example, when J. B. Phillips renders 'greet one another with a holy kiss' at Romans 16:16 with 'give one another a hearty handshake all around' (Nida 1964: 160).

In translation studies over recent decades, though, there has been an increasing recognition that a translation needs to take into consideration more than just the linguistic and the relation to the source text and its culture. Which is why in many domains the very notion of 'translation' is so often now giving way to an alternative concept, that of 'localisation'. The very term itself has been shifted to incorporate a different relation to place which focuses on the target or receiving culture and prioritises the preservation of local differences in linguistic and cultural reference.

References

ADAMS, Robert M. 1973. *Proteus: His Lies, His Truth*. New York: W. W. Norton.

AKASHI, Motoko. 2018. 'Translator Celebrity: Investigating Haruki Murakami's Visibility as a Translator'. *Celebrity Studies*.

ALBERTAZZI, Silvia. 1993. *Translating India: Travel and Cross-Cultural Transference in Post-Colonial Indian Fiction in English*. Bologna: CLUEB.

APTER, Emily. 2006. *The Translation Zone: A New Comparative Literature*. Princeton, NJ and Oxford: Princeton University Press.

ARMITSTEAD, Claire. 2018. 'Lost in (Mis)translation? English Take on Korean Novel has Critics Up in Arms'. *The Guardian*, 15 January. Online at www.theguardian.com/books/booksblog/2018/jan/15/lost-in-mistranslation-english-take-on-korean-novel-has-critics-up-in-arms.

BAKER, Mona (ed.). 1998. *Routledge Encyclopedia of Translation Studies*. London: Routledge.

BASSNETT, Susan. 2002. *Translation Studies*, 3rd edn. London: Routledge.

CAMBONI, Marina, Andrea Carosso, Sonia Di Loreto and Marco Mariano (eds). 2011. *Translating America: The Circulation of Narratives, Commodities, and Ideas between Italy, Europe, and the United States*. Berne and New York: Peter Lang.

CATFORD, J. C. 1965. *A Linguistic Theory of Translation: An Essay in Applied Linguistics*. London: Oxford University Press.

CHANDRAN, Mini, and Suchitra Mathur (eds). 2014. *Textual Travels: Theory and Practice of Translation in India*. New Delhi: Routledge India.

CHEUNG, Martha P. Y. (ed.). 2006. *An Anthology of Chinese Discourse on Translation, Volume 1: From Earliest Times to the Buddhist Project*. Manchester: St Jerome.

—— and Robert Neather (eds). 2017. *An Anthology of Chinese Discourse on Translation, Volume 2: From the Late Twelfth Century to 1800*. London: Routledge, 2017.

CHEW, Shirley (ed.). 2015. *Moving Worlds* 15 (1) (Translating Southeast Asia: Special Issue).

CONOLLY-SMITH, Peter. 2004. *Translating America: An Immigrant Press Visualizes American Popular Culture, 1895–1918.* Washington, DC: Smithsonian Books.

CRESSWELL, Tim. 2009. 'Place'. *International Encyclopedia of Human Geography* (Rob Kitchin and Nigel Thrift eds), 8: 169–77. Oxford: Elsevier.

CRONIN, Michael. 1996. *Translating Ireland: Translation, Languages, Cultures.* Cork: Cork University Press.

——. 2000. *Across the Lines: Travel, Language and Translation.* Cork: Cork University Press.

——. 2003. *Translation and Globalization.* New York: Routledge.

——. 2006. *Translation and Identity.* London: Routledge.

——. 2013. *Translation in the Digital Age.* New York: Routledge.

EPSTEIN, B. J. 2012. *Translating Expressive Language in Children's Literature: Problems and Solutions.* Oxford: Peter Lang.

FAN, Jiayang. 2018. 'Han Kang and the Complexity of Translation'. *New Yorker*, 15 January. Available online at www.newyorker.com/magazine/2018/01/15/han-kang-and-the-complexity-of-translation.

FRIEL, Brian. 1981. *Translations.* London: Faber and Faber.

GRAVES, Robert. 2010. *Translating Rome* (Robert Cummings ed.). Manchester: Carcanet.

HOWLAND, Douglas R. 2002. *Translating the West: Language and Political Reason in Nineteenth-Century Japan.* Honolulu: University of Hawaii Press.

HUNG, Eva, and Judy Wakabayashi (eds). 2005. *Asian Translation Traditions.* Manchester and Northampton, MA: St. Jerome.

ITALIANO, Federico. 2016. *Translation and Geography.* New York: Routledge.

KOTHARI, Rita. 2003. *Translating India: The Cultural Politics of English.* Manchester and Northampton, MA: St. Jerome.

KERSHAW, Angela, and Gabriela Saldanha. 2013. 'Introduction: Global Landscapes of Translation'. *Translation Studies* 6 (2): 135–49.

LEFEVERE, André. 1977. *Translating Literature: The German Tradition from Luther to Rosenzweig*. Assen: Van Gorcum.

—— (ed.). 1992. *Translation / History / Culture: A Sourcebook*. London: Routledge.

LUIS, William, and Julio Rodríguez-Luis (eds). 1991. *Translating Latin America: Culture as Text*. Binghamton, NY: Center for Research in Translation, State University of New York at Binghamton.

LUO XUANMIN and He Yuanjian (eds). 2009. *Translating China*. Bristol and Buffalo, NY: Multilingual Matters.

MINTZ, Alan L. 2001. *Translating Israel: Contemporary Hebrew Literature and its Reception in America*. Syracuse, NY: Syracuse University Press.

MUNDAY, Jeremy. 2001. *Introducing Translation Studies: Theories and Applications*. London: Routledge.

NIDA, Eugene A. 1964. *Toward a Science of Translating: With Special Reference to Principles and Procedures involved in Bible Translating*. Leiden and Boston, MA: Brill.

PENNYCOOK, Alastair, and Emi Otsuji. 2015. *Metrolingualism: Language in the City*. London: Routledge.

PYM, Anthony. 1996. 'Venuti's Visibility'. *Target* 8 (2): 165–77.

ROSA, Alexandra Assis. 2012. 'Translating Place: Linguistic Variation in Translation'. *Word and Text* 2 (2): 75–97.

ROSE, Emily. 2018. 'Surmounting the 'Insurmountable' Challenges of Translating a Transgender Memoir' in Duncan Large (et al. eds), *Untranslatability: Interdisciplinary Perspectives*. New York: Routledge.

SCHLEIERMACHER, Friedrich. 2012[1813]. 'On the Different Methods of Translating' (Susan Bernofsky trans.) in Lawrence Venuti (ed.), *The Translation Studies Reader*, 3rd edn. New York: Routledge, pp. 43–63.

Sᴄɪᴀʀʀɪɴᴏ, Chiara. 2005. *Translating Italy: Notes on Irish Poets Reading Italian Poetry*. Rome: Aracne.

Sɪᴍᴏɴ, Sherry. 2012. *Cities in Translation: Intersections of Language and Memory*. New York: Routledge.

——. 2018. 'Space' in Sue-Ann Harding and Ovidi Carbonell Cortés (eds), *Routledge Handbook of Translation and Culture*. New York: Routledge, pp. 97–111.

—— (ed.). 2016. *Speaking Memory: How Translation Shapes City Life*. Montreal: McGill-Queen's University Press.

Sᴘɪᴠᴀᴋ, Gayatri Chakravorty. 2012. 'The Politics of Translation' in Lawrence Venuti (ed.), *The Translation Studies Reader*, 3rd edn. London: Routledge, pp. 312–30.

Tᴏʟᴀɴsᴋɪ, Jon. 2003. 'International Case Studies' in Colin Lawson (ed.), *The Cambridge Companion to the Orchestra*. Cambridge: Cambridge University Press, pp. 126–54.

Vᴇɴᴜᴛɪ, Lawrence. 1995. *The Translator's Invisibility: A History of Translation*. London: Routledge.

ᴠᴏɴ Fʟᴏᴛᴏw, Luise, and Reingard M. Nischik (eds). 2007. *Translating Canada*. Ottawa: University of Ottawa Press.

Yɪ-Fᴜ Tᴜᴀɴ. 1977. *Space and Place: The Perspective of Experience*. Minneapolis and London: University of Minnesota Press.

Notes on Contributors

Lucy Hughes-Hallett's biography of Gabriele d'Annunzio, *The Pike* (2013), won all three of the UK's most prestigious prizes for non-fiction—the Samuel Johnson Prize, the Costa Biography Award and the Duff Cooper Prize. In 2017 she published her first novel, *Peculiar Ground,* spanning three centuries, moving between an English stately home and Berlin and combining all the pleasures of historical fiction with a timely investigation of migration and exclusion. Lucy lives in London and Suffolk, and travels regularly to India. She is a Fellow of the Royal Society of Literature. The piece was written in the flat watery landscape of coastal Suffolk.

Pia Ghosh-Roy grew up in India, and now lives in Cambridge, UK. Her fiction, poetry and essays have been published in the UK, US, India and New Zealand. She won the 2017 Hamlin Garland Award for her story 'The Resurrection of Rakesh Sharma'. Her other stories have been placed in, and shortlisted and longlisted for several prizes, including the Aestas Fabula Press Competition, Bath Short Story Award, Brighton Prize, Berlin Writing Prize, Fish Short Story Competition and Hourglass Literary Magazine Short Story

Contest. Pia is working on her first novel and a collection of short stories. Pia wrote her story in Cambridge.

Tiffany Atkinson is a poet and literary critic. Her poems are published widely in journals and anthologies, and her first collection, *Kink and Particle* (Seren, 2006) was a Poetry Book Society Recommendation, and winner of the Jerwood Aldeburgh First Collection Prize. Her second, *Catulla et al* (Bloodaxe, 2011) was shortlisted for the Wales Book of the Year, and her third collection, *So Many Moving Parts*, (Bloodaxe 2014) was a Poetry Book Society Recommendation and winner of the Roland Mathias Poetry Prize. Her forthcoming collection, which explores medicine and experiences of healthcare, was the winner of the 2014 Medicine Unboxed Creative Prize. Tiffany gives regular readings and workshops across the UK and internationally, and is Professor of Creative Writing (Poetry), University of East Anglia. Tiffany wrote her poems at various locations.

Parni Ray is a writer and curator from Kolkata. An alumnus of the Department of Arts and Aesthetics, Jawaharlal Nehru University, New Delhi and a former curator at the Students' Biennale at the Kochi-Muziris Biennale, her solo curatorial venture *Soft City* opened at Range Gallery, Kolkata, in 2015. Currently a student at the Royal College of Art, her research and curatorial interests revolve around narrative image-making. Parni shot her photographs in Norwich.

Vesna Goldworthy is an internationally bestselling and prize-winning writer, academic and broadcaster. She moved to Britain from Serbia in her twenties and writes in English, her third language. Her recent work includes two novels: *Gorsky* (2015)—a reworking of *The Great Gatsby* featuring Russians in London, which was translated into fifteen languages, long-listed for the Baileys Prize and serialised on the BBC, as well as being the Waterstones

Book of the Year and the *New York Times* editors' choice—and *Monsieur Ka* (2018), the story of Anna Karenina's son Sergei. Vesna has family links with Kolkata going back to mid-1800s. Vesna wrote 'Hare Street' in London soon after her first visit to Kolkata in January 2016.

Somrita Ganguly is a professor, writer and literary translator. Currently affiliated with Brown University, Rhode Island, as a Fulbright Doctoral Research Fellow, she has taught British Literature to undergraduates in Kolkata and Delhi, and was Poet-in-Residence at Arcs-of-a-Circle Artists' Residency, Bombay. Somrita wrote her piece in Kolkata.

Currently writing a libretto for the Welsh National Opera and a collection of short stories for HarperCollins, former television producer and broadcast journalist **Shreya Sen-Handley** is also kept busy by her children (human and canine), her creative-writing workshops for a wide range of organisations including the Universities of Nottingham and Cambridge, her regular prattle on BBC and Notts TV, her occasional forays into illustrating, her plentiful articles for international media including the *National Geographic Traveller* and *Hindustan Times*, and the fallout from her recent UNESCO Cities of Literature–endorsed memoir, *Memoirs of My Body* (HarperCollins). Shreya wrote her piece in Sherwood Forest, looking out over a thousand-year-old wall listed in the Domesday Book, and an orchard in which the Byrons duelled.

Sreedevi Nair is Associate Professor and Head of the Department of English, NSS College for Women, Neeramankara, Thiruvananthapuram, Kerala. During her time at the British Centre for Literary Translation, she undertook independent research entitled 'Sita's Sorrow: When Malayali Women Retell The Ramayana.' Sreedevi wrote her piece in Norwich.

Sarah Bower is a novelist, short-story writer and teacher of creative writing who lives and works in Norwich. Her story was inspired by a card she found in her hotel bedroom in Kolkata when she visited the city as part of the Writing Places project in 2017. It contained a list of prompts aimed at business travellers, and she knew the moment she saw it that it would provide her with a framework for a story. She wrote the story back in Norwich, with her Kolkata notebook at her side.

Mandakranta Sen is a prominent voice in contemporary Bengali literature. Her literary engagement spans various genres: she has authored nineteen collections of poems, eight novels, two volumes of short fiction and a book of essays. She works as a translator, playwright, lyricist, composer, cover designer and editor of a little magazine, and her work has been widely translated. Mandakranta wrote her poems in Kolkata.

Chirodeep Chaudhuri is the author of the critically feted *A Village In Bengal: Photographs and an Essay*, a result of his thirteen-year-long engagement with his ancestral village in West Bengal, and his family's nearly two-century-old tradition of Durga Puja. His most recent book, *With Great Truth & Regard*, documents the history of the manual typewriter in India.Chirodeep's work documents the urban landscape and he has produced a range of projects including *Bombay Clocks, The One-Rupee Entrepreneur, The Commuters* and *In the City, a Library* among others. His work has been featured in some of the most important publications on Bombay. He lives in Bombay, dividing his time between his various projects and teaching assignments. Chirodeep shot his photographs in Mumbai, at the People's Free Reading Room & Library.

Jerry Pinto has spent his life in Bombay, Mumbai, Momoi, Mhamai, Bambai. He says, 'One of the toughest parts of my job as a writer is the challenge of trying to define myself in a hundred words but it is always worth giving it a shot to see whether I can manage to create a meaningful précis of my life that will fulfil the needs of a book designer in some other part of the world, simply as a test of how far my patience can take me when I am writing something no reader will ever bother to read.' Jerry wrote his piece in Mahim, Mumbai.

Paramita Satpathy Tripathy is an influential voice in Odia Literature. She has published seven short story collections, two novels and one novella. Her works have been extensively translated into English and a range of other Indian languages. She had received, among other awards, the Sahitya Akademi Award in 2016 for her collection of novellas *Prapti*. Paramita wrote her story in Bhubaneswar.

Kate Griffin is Associate Programme Director, National Centre for Writing, with a particular focus on international writing and translation, working wth partners in the Far East, Asia and Europe. She was a judge for the Independent Foreign Fiction Prize from 2006 to 2010 and for the Singapore Literature Prize in 2018. In the 1990s she lived and worked in Brussels and Moscow, and she continues to travel as often as possible. She has a photography blog at kategriffin.org. 'Sacred Plants' was written at the Old Rectory, Rosary Road, Norwich. The photographs were taken in and around Rougham in Norfolk, Bawali in Bengal and the Botanic Gardens in Calcutta.

Sirsho Bandopadhyay lived in Kolkata almost all his life, except for a few years in Germany. A journalist for the past 30 years, he has worked for newspapers, radio, television and online sites. He began writing fiction in 2015, and has published seven books in Bengali—four novels, two biographies and a collection of features. He writes stories for all the major Bengali publications. An avid traveller, he is also an enthusiastic photographer. Sirsho wrote his story in Kolkata.

Anjali Joseph has written three novels—*Saraswati Park*, *Another Country* and *The Living* which appeared in 2016. She studied English at Trinity College, Cambridge, and has worked as a journalist, a trainee accountant, a French teacher and, more recently, a creative-writing tutor. She has lived in Bombay, Leamington Spa, Paris, London and Guwahati, and now lives in Oxfordshire and teaches on the MSt in Creative Writing at Oxford. 'Everlasting Lucifer', an excerpt from her fourth novel-in-progress, was longlisted for the *Sunday Times* Short Story Award in 2017; another excerpt has appeared in the anthology *Others*. Anjali wrote the piece in Uzan Bazar, Guwahati.

Sarah Hickson captures images that resonate with the feeling of our shared humanity. A photographer based in London but always travelling, her practice explores the relationship between people and place through visual narratives of emotional connection that empathise with the beauty, fragility and resilience of the human spirit. Her recent work explores displacement and migration, the power of the arts to cross boundaries and create community, and the expressive qualities of the physical body. Her collaborations with artists have led her to a deeper enquiry into the intersection between photography, creative process, and live performance. She has had solo exhibitions in NYC, London, Paris, and Bamako and has been published widely in the international press. Sarah wrote her piece and edited the selection of images in London.

Samit Basu is an Indian novelist best known for his fantasy and science fiction work. His first novel, *The Simoqin Prophecies*, (Penguin India, 2003), was the first book in the bestselling Gameworld trilogy and marked the beginning of Indian English fantasy writing. Samit's superhero novels *Turbulence* and *Resistance* (Titan Books, 2012/13) were published in the UK and the US to rave reviews. Samit also writes for younger readers (the Adventures of Stoob series) and in other media: screenplays, short stories and comics. He was born in Calcutta and now lives in Delhi. Samit wrote his story in Delhi.

Duncan Large is Professor of European Literature and Translation, University of East Anglia (Norwich); and Academic Director, British Centre for Literary Translation. He has authored and edited five books on Nietzsche and German philosophy as well as two Nietzsche translations (Oxford World's Classics), and a French translation (Sarah Kofman's *Nietzsche and Metaphor*, Continuum). He is co-editor of *Untranslatability: Interdisciplinary Perspectives* (Routledge 2018); and with Alan D Schrift, also General Editor of *The Complete Works of Friedrich Nietzsche* (Stanford University Press). Duncan wrote his piece at his two desks: his office at UEA and his home office in Cambridge.